Siren's Score

C.K. Malavasic

Published by C.K. Malavasic, 2022.

Copyright

Also by C.K. Malavasic

Siren's Score
Containment Web

Watch for more at https://ckmalavasic.com.

Dedication

To those relatives and friends who encouraged a young author to write fantastical tales but aren't here to see one published. They laid the foundation for this collection.

To the relatives, teachers, and friends who graciously stepped into this adventure, learning new skills and techniques along the way and seeing this through.

For those readers who will pick up this work and slip into the world within.

Siren's Flood

Siren's Storm

Siren's Shield

Siren's Fury

Siren's Song

Part I
Siren's Flood

She looked down on the Forbidden Forest encircling her home and prison of twenty years. The black mist wafted through the trees forming grotesque outlines. If anyone was so stupid to enter her forest, they wouldn't see the real monsters creeping up on them until too late to defend themselves.

She remembered the celebrations when the Black Mage had been defeated by the Order of Knights years ago. The fireworks bursting over the city and the dances.

The kind boy from next door who gave her a kiss. Her first.

Mary hadn't known it would be her only kiss.

When she joined in the lottery she never thought she'd be chosen for this life.

The crowds cheered as each person drew fabulous prizes. The blacksmith got his weight in gold. He'd swung his beefy arms above his head in victory when Mary walked up for her turn. She wished for a horse so she could explore the world.

The chief of the lottery motioned her forward as he crossed off the blacksmith's reward.

The barrel dwarfed her. It rotated with loud rattling to mix up the inch long tokens of various colors, materials and symbols for her pick.

Mary's hand shook as she reached into the barrel to pick a token.

She pulled it out and looked at the black token with a bat on it. She didn't recognize what prize group it belonged to.

She turned to the chief and offered up the token to learn her reward.

He looked at the token, then cupped her hand over it, "A special audience with the king!"

Mary looked up at him in puzzlement. The king didn't offer up audiences.

If she'd known then what she did now, she'd have tossed the token away.

That audience changed her life for the worse.

She'd been ten years old.

The king, a bear of a man, towered over her with cold grey eyes. His red hair hung in braids thicker than her wrist, from a golden crown encrusted with rubies and diamonds.

He'd told her the kingdom had a protection spell to ward off outside evil forces. However, it required an evil force inside the kingdom. The token contained a spell. It choose the next evil power when the old one died.

She became the next evil.

Within a day she was shoved into the tower of the Black Mage and sealed in with magic.

The king looked at Mary with contempt as she struck the pale blue walls with tiny fists, "You will only break free of the seal once you have enough power, evil one."

Then the king left, laughing cruelly.

Hatred fueled her for ten years until she burst the seal in an explosion of water, flooding parts of four kingdoms.

The forest before that moment had been vivid green and sunlit, recovered from its time under the Black Mage. However, it quickly succumbed to her magics.

She became Siren, sorceress of water.

Mary knew she was used to power the defenses, but she didn't care anymore. Soon she'd break those defenses and allow evil from outside to flood this kingdom with unspeakable horrors.

The stream of heroes increased, just like before the Dark Mage had been slain. Mary knew it would be a matter of time before she joined him in death.

The final phase of the spell would take all of her energy. Energy she couldn't waste on the line of heroes she saw in the distance marching her way.

The king must have summoned heroes of the other kingdoms to slay her. That advantage of the wall aided him. All good may pass into and out of the kingdom, while evil outside had to stay out and evil inside prevented from leaving.

Screams echoed from the edge of the forest as the first of the heroes began their assault.

Mary swept inside the tower, willing the doors to her balcony closed behind her.

She crossed into the spell circle, picking up her dress train so it didn't drag through the salt lines. She paused briefly to rub the pendent at the base of her throat. The last item from her old life still held a vestige of the power her father placed in it.

She stood in the center of the three concentric circles, composing herself while she gathered her strength. This would stand as her last defiance to the rules imposed upon her.

Her words rose in incantation the Dark Mage nearly perfected when he'd fallen. Her touches finalized it to a suitable form against the king.

Dying shrieks of her guards and monsters rose steadily up the tower.

She whispered the last words when the door to her room shattered.

Mary felt the power drain away from her, as she turned her head to look at the one who breached her tower.

He dressed not in the normal gold armor of heroes, instead he donned dark grey, piped with silver. A dark grey cloak edged in black fur flared open as he looked around the tower. A silver helm protected his head and his nose.

He grinned at her then, his reddish brown beard parting to white teeth.

"Well, I certainly didn't think you'd do it."

Mary shook from head to toe with chill, but her voice rang imperiously, "Do what, pray tell?"

"You just reinforced the barrier."

She scowled at him, "You jest."

He sheathed his sword, "Then look outside. See for yourself."

She didn't fall for the trick. If she broke the circle, the spell would drop.

"Suspicious," he leaned against the doorway, "However, that spell you cast will take more from you the longer you stand there."

"I don't believe a hero. Not after what King Terlon did to me."

"What did he do?"

The inner ring of salts vanished and Mary struggled for breath.

When she regained her composure, she glared at him, "A hero would sacrifice anyone for the greater good. Slay anyone. I took a bloody token that marked me as the next evil."

"So you decided to take revenge on the kingdom by using the spell they left behind?"

She snarled, "Who are you to judge me? The prince?"

The man laughed, "As if pretty boy would ever rouse himself to pick an apple, much less take on an evil."

The second line drove her to her knees when it vanished.

She shook with the effort to stay kneeling.

He looked less amused, "Come out of there, girl. You gain nothing."

"Nothing? That is what a hero would say. Stop the spell, join us. No. I will not be fooled. They set me up as a sacrifice and they will get it. I modified the spell left by the Dark Mage."

The man went still, "You what?"

She chuckled evilly at him, "No spell here worked for me to breach the seal," she peeled off her glove slowly, "I had to experiment."

His eyes behind the helm slits widened, as a shadow darkened the archway behind him.

"This is what has become of me. The king sealed me in until I either died trying to breach the seal or shattered it."

Blackened skin sprinkled with white ridges of scars covered her entire hand. She worked at fire spells until she lost the use of her left hand. Then she turned to earth spells, before she nearly died, frozen in stone. The wind shredded her face so it no longer looked beautiful. The welts made her look older than her age and horrible. She'd been tempted to shatter the mirrors so she didn't need to look upon her own visage.

"So hero, I found water to be more malleable, but had to craft my own spells to use it. When I saw the spell, I knew it wasn't complete. I saw the sacrifice could be turned to bring down the accursed barrier."

He strode to the edge of the third ring, "Is this worth it?"

"When I returned to my village, my mother and father were long dead by grief, my best friend screamed at me while her husband tried to slay me, and my old teacher tried to bind me with his last breath. This is worth it to tell the cruel king choosing a child to be the next evil without her consent is not righteous. It is evil, and evil begets evil."

The last ring began to shimmer.

She looked down her nose at the hero, hard to do while kneeling, but she managed, "The king already put the token of evil into the barrel. I do this to protect the next child from being tortured with this life. They may get the horse instead and ride from this dark kingdom without looking back," Mary collapsed to her hands and knees, her hair dangling in thick, brown, gnarled ropes, "I'd rather die as the last evil of this land than to see another innocent forced to decide to suicide or take power to be free."

"They don't suicide."

She laughed, crying at him, "Look in the cellar and see how many died by self inflicted wounds or poison. Then claim that."

The ring vanished and her breath fled her. She collapsed upon the stone she crossed so many times in frustration. Now she wouldn't see it ever again as her vision went dark.

"What did you change?" The hero demanded and then shook her, "Tell me!"

She thought bitterly, You wouldn't even know what I did even if I explained it. No one would. I used my magic to destroy the token in the barrel. To make it dust.

Howls cut through the tower, inhuman and cruel.

"You would do this to us? To destroy all for one child?"

Her breath wheezed in and she whispered, "That is what makes me evil. I would damn the world for one child's innocence."

Then she swept away and under the darkness.

***

Her breath gasped in, making her jerk up.

She sat on a soft pallet which crinkled under her as she shook with coughs, her lungs struggling to breath.

"Here, sip this," clawed hands placed a cup into her hands.

She looked up into a lesser demon's eyes.

"So I did end up in hell," she wheezed.

"Hardly," a man towered over the demon, "But after what you went through, I hope this looks heavenly."

He dressed in pure black robes edged with white minx. Black embroidery trailed over his shoulders downward in the form of dragons. His blond hair started to go silver at the temples, and his blue eyes crinkled into laugh wrinkles.

"Who are you?" Mary asked.

"King Gerard. I'm the one who saved you from the tower and that so called hero."

"I don't understand," she hacked for several seconds.

"The Hundred Kingdoms sent thousands of heroes to defeat evil which continually sprouted in Mekrone, your kingdom. We couldn't understand how evil seemed to return when it never crossed into the realm. When I arrived to the top of the tower you said you would damn the whole kingdom for a child. Would you please explain," he smiled wryly, "After you have a few sips so my personal healer doesn't claw me."

"As if I could scratch your skin," the demon huffed indignantly, his black claws scraping noisily on his white ram horns, his skin changing from pale red to vivid purple, "tough like your head."

Mary sipped, found it plain tea. No magic. No poison.

She sat before a captive audience who wanted to know her story, and she didn't need to hunt them down.

She explained the tokens and what made her become Siren. How she corrupted the spell to bring down the barrier rather than cast as the Dark Mage left it.

King Gerard stared at the wall, his gaze unhappy, when she finished.

"Sacrificing children to prevent evil from crossing into their lands. Genius yet unspeakably cruel. To turn their final moments of victory into one more defeat," he stood, brushed off his robe more in habit than need, "I'll report this to the Gathering. Please recover your strength, young lady."

"Why? What would I recover for?"

He looked at her, "Why, to take down the corrupt and evil king of your land. You control the water of the land. You can help us bring him to justice."

Mary blinked at him, "What?"

The demon chided the king, "She exhausted all her powers breaking a wall no evil army could and now you want her to attack her former king? She needs three weeks of rest at least."

"Which is why I said she should recover, dear friend. I'll be back," he swept out.

"Drink. Then sleep," the demon muttered, "Foolish king."

King Gerard's amused voice drifted back to Mary, "I heard that."

***

She took six weeks to recover. The lesser demon, Trikic, used his magics to heal her. He managed to turn her blackened skin to match the pale scars, soften the skin on her face, and with the help of a camp maid, brushed and braided her hair back.

Mary hardly recognized the person she stared at in the mirror. She looked neither Siren nor Mary. Someone between.

King Gerard presented her a dark blue robe with black minx fur. She felt like she was human again, and not an evil sorceress.

Trikic chirped as he came into her tent, "The Gathering wish your appearance, Mary."

She nodded, standing. She walked out after Trikic towards the command tent.

Ducking under the flap, she straightened to her full height of six feet and looked over the representatives of the Hundred Kingdoms.

There were so many different species, sizes and bright colors. A glittering hummingbird sized female fairy sat on the shoulder of a male orge, speaking in whispers.

"Lady Mary, please come sit here," King Gerard indicated a chair beside him.

She carefully wove her way to his side, "King Gerard."

She sat politely, silence sweeping the group and eyes swinging to her.

"King Silva, would you start?" King Gerard indicated a tall lizard sitting on his haunches.

"Of course," the lizard rolled his 's', "We are here because we found the spell that powered the barrier of Mekrone is not as the king of the land claimed. Lady Mary, known in Mekrone as Siren, brought done the barrier. If she hadn't, only part of her power would maintain the barrier. The rest has been siphoned off."

Mary looked at him in surprise. She hadn't read that in the spell.

"The barrier linked to a reservoir in case there no spell caster could power it," King Silva murmured, "Yet every time an evil is chosen immediately on the death of the prior one. When we tapped the reservoir, none of the power it should contain remained."

Mary felt her heart skip a beat. Where did the power go?

King Silva continued, "The true evil of this kingdom consumed it. It sheltered its feeding grounds from all others by sacrificing angry children to its power base. Until Lady Mary shattered the barrier no one could scry inside Mekrone. Many of the oracles and prophets suddenly had visions of danger, a raging inferno that will explode from within Mekrone. One scryist screamed of winged death before dying."

Mary swallowed as whispers and murmurs followed.

"Lady Mary. Please take the floor and tell us of what lead to your spectacular entrance upon our awareness," King Silva nodded to her.

She stood, "Thank you for your consideration. Before I became Siren, I was a little girl, ten years of age. When the Dark Mage was vanquished by the heroes of the time, the Barrel of Fortunes was brought out. Each resident took a token which is supposed to be a reward for surviving the dark years. The man before me got his weight in gold. I hoped for a horse, instead I drew a black token with a bat etched on it. The Chief of the Lottery said it was an audience with the king. It was a death sentence. The king explained to me the token chose me to be the next evil so the barrier may remain up. He imprisoned me in the tower of the Dark Mage with a seal only a powerful caster could breach. I remember he laughed the whole time I screamed to be let out.

"I spent ten years in that tower, finding the bones of those who died inside the seal either by age or their own hands, the journals of those who succeeded in breaching the seal to become their age's evil and the monsters breed throughout time. Magic did not come easily to me but I managed to burst the seal with a greater water elemental."

King Silva hissed, "You summoned a greater elemental?"

"I did. My affinity is with water, which is why I am called Siren. I drowned my enemies while I tried to learn the magics behind the barrier spell."

"Drowned champions of our kingdoms," the fairy screamed, taking to the air, "Killed brothers and husbands."

"Yes. I did. If you need to take my crimes out of my hide, you may do so after dealing with the corruption at the core of my kingdom."

"You would allow us to try and punish you?" The fairy backed up in shock.

"I know my actions caused great suffering both within and without. I will pay for my misdeeds. I knew this when I took up the role and fought to complete the spell with my modifications to bring it down," she looked at the fairy, "Hundreds of children were killed to power that barrier and none of you noticed. You could pass in and out easily, yet took no actions to save children forced into slavery. I used the knowledge that my successor would be tortured to the same life as me, to fight. To save her and a number of children who would get that token and vanish from their parents. Mine died of grief while I was caged."

She looked over them, saw the shamed looks and averted eyes, "I survived until I could sacrifice my life to save my successor. To bring down the barrier. I fully expected the hero who breached the tower to kill me before the spell took. You know that there is something far more rotten at the core of my kingdom and once dealt with, you can take the price of your champions dead at my hands from me."

King Gerard spoke up, "Lady Mary will be brought to trial. We need her because of her connection to the waters of Mekrone. If fire rages, she would be able to call the rains and the rivers to aid us. We were blind to the troubles, but no longer. We have massed our armies so we need to strike."

Mary sat down, shivering at the viciousness in his voice. She did not want to be on the wrong side of his blade.

He stood, "Whatever winged death is going to rise, we need to face it with the fury of righteousness."

"She is evil," the fairy shrieked at Mary, "She will betray us."

King Silva snickered at the fairy, "She acted far better than you, Speaker of Fairies. Though we cannot ignore this problem."

Mary nodded, "I understand. What would you wish of me?"

She was fortunate to be alive, sitting here to plot against her former king. If they needed assurances, she would give them. To take down his evil would be well worth having her power taken away. It had done nothing to bring her happiness.

Silence reigned as the gathered leaders looked around, unsure of what to say.

King Gerard shook his head, "None of you thought on this?"

"I expected her to demur," King Silva looked at Mary, "You are surprising."

"Do not think me defanged. I have been accustomed to answer only to myself. If needed I will lie, manipulate, and murder to accomplish my goals. My goal coincides with yours in this."

King Gerard raised a hand to stop a debate, "My element is earth. I can use my power to shackle hers until we need her."

An explosion of voices greeted this as Mary stared at King Gerard.

"Are you certain?" her voice low and full of threat.

He smiled at her, his eyes flashing with something darker, "I assure you, Lady Mary, I can handle whatever you dish out."

She raised an eyebrow, "We shall see, won't we."

***

Mary looked down at the valley, itching to unleash a spell, but Gerard's power chained her.

Her skin felt like stone again. A claustrophobic feeling, made more so by the resisting army.

They had stalled the armies of the Hundred Kingdoms at the ravine leading into the capital.

She wanted to cast a flood spell to clear the way.

"Calm down," Gerard murmured, "We will breach."

"I could clear them in a few moments," she hissed when his power clamped down on her, "Ease up."

"No. I will not have you flood the city."

She sneered, "It would make our enemy take to offense."

He looked at her with disapproval, "Trust me. You need to save your power. Relax."

"I hate being stone," she slumped in the saddle, scowling at the armies, "I could call some of my surviving minions."

"Don't sulk, either," his eyes turned towards the sky suddenly.

She followed his gaze.

Her mouth dropped open.

Ten huge black scaled dragons plummeted towards the army of the Hundred Kingdoms.

"You're right. Bring them down," Gerard snapped as the beasts scorched the middle of the army, killing hundreds with each pass of flame.

His power fled from her.

She began chanting, eyes focused on the dragons.

Winged death. The dead prophet spoke truly.

The rocks on either side of the ravine cracked then spurted fountains, the water shooting skyward.

She raised her hands, the water forming giant hands.

The dragons screamed before she clasped her hands together, the water hands crushing them.

She gave into her urges and brought her hands back then threw them out. The liquid hands pitched the dead bodies over the city to strike the mountain at its back.

She smirked, glad she finally got to kill something.

Then the ground shook, spooking her horse.

The horse reared, tossing her backwards and off.

Strong arms circled her, halting her fall.

Gerard shouted as he controlled his horse with his legs, pulling her unto his lap, "Hold!"

A roar bellowed over that land.

A figure appeared on the top of the ravine, growing in size.

The king of Mekrone.

"You should have died, you selfish child," his voice struck terror into Mary, throwing her back into her childhood, staring up at him when he pronounced her condemnation, "My children are far more valuable than you."

Gerard shouted, "You lie, King Terlon. You sacrificed innocence to horde power."

She shivered fighting her memories of screaming at the seal, in pain from the fire spells, in despair.

The king transformed into a massive dragon, black red-edged scales glistening from the collapsed water hands. His wings snapped open, before he took to the air.

"I have become unbeatable, little king. Not even your tactics will save the Hundred Kingdoms. I will burn your kingdoms to ash and dance upon your bones."

"Summon your elemental," something shook her, "Summon your elemental!"

The dragon reared back its head, laughing.

Arrows flew up at it but skittered off his scales.

A hand gripped her chin, forced her head around.

Lips covered hers.

She jerked back, stared at Gerard in shock.

"Summon your elemental."

"Water cannot harm me anymore," the voice thundered above them.

She whipped her head around and up to her enemy.

Water swirled upward in vicious spikes, the air chilling as she focused her spell. Icy spears to take down the dragon.

The dragon breathed on the spikes, sending billowing steam around it.

"You cannot harm me," the voice boomed, forcing the steam to part with each word.

Mary scrambled mentally for a solution as the dragon inhaled again.

Somehow she had to protect the water until it could kill the dragon.

She looked at Gerard, "Shield my elemental with stone."

She raised the elemental in front of them, a tower of water.

Stone plates circled the water, spiraling in a complex pattern.

The dragon opened its mouth wide.

She sent her elemental up into his throat.

He thrashed in the air, choking on the stone clad elemental as it filled his body. She could see the stone smoking from the heat of his breath, but her water didn't evaporated.

"I read you dragons die when your fire goes out," she smirked at his pain filled and frightened eyes, "Enjoy your drink."

His body exploded, showering down fiery bits.

Stone built above her, deflecting the debris.

"Secure the city," Gerard ordered as he brought down his stone shield.

The army marched out, healers rushing to the wounded that could be saved.

She won. Defeated her original enemy.

The fairy shoved suddenly into her face, "Now you will be tried."

King Silva moved to them on all fours, his armor clinking softly, "Not so fast, Speaker of Fairies. We all have debts she needs to pay."

"Let us ensure the city has no other dangers, then we can use the general assembly hall to discuss how to make everyone whole."

"She can't be allowed to escape," the fairy snapped, "She killed many of my kingdoms champions."

Sand sprinkled into Mary's eyes.

She tried to raise her hand to brush it away but she lost all her strength, her body going limp.

"Damn you," Mary's head lolled back onto Gerard's shoulder so she looked up at him, "Sleeping sand."

***

When she woke, she wore multiple pieces of jewelry. She had so many rings on each finger that they acted like a gauntlet. Bracelets marched up her arms to stop below her elbow, where above armbands took over up to her shoulders. She tossed aside the blankets to find her ankles jangling with anklets and her toes clicked with rings.

She stood, spotted a mirror and went to see her face, fearing what she would find.

Her ears were clasped by many ear cuffs of different colors and dangled two sets of earrings. A dozen pendents circled her neck.

When she tried to pull one of the rings from her finger it wouldn't budge.

"Each adornment," Gerard appeared in the mirror, standing behind her, when she looked up, "represents a kingdom you owe a hero debt to."

"I thought I was to be tried and executed."

"That would be unfair to the other kingdoms, as some practice a lifetime service as punishment. When you pay your debt to the kingdom it belongs to, the jewelry piece will vanish. When all pieces vanish, you will be free to chose what you want to do."

She rankled someone bound her with seals. Like the one she breached to escape the tower.

"How do I pay the debt?"

"You will be a heroine of the Hundred Kingdoms. Each time you solve a problem, slay a rampaging beast, stop a war, a piece of your debt will be paid."

"So I have to pay back the service of every hero I ever killed," she regretted each murder now. She'd never be free.

"No. Each kingdom agreed that you saved us from a fate that would leave all our kingdoms in ruins."

She turned, looked at him, "Even the Fairies?"

He smiled, "Yes. Though I think your debt to them will be the hardest to pay even with the reduction."

"I would think no one would want Siren as their hero."

"We want Lady Mary as our heroine. She defended a child from the same fate she suffered."

She scowled at him, "Do you always win arguments?"

He smiled, "I always get what I want. If you would get dressed in your gear, I want you to see your noble steed."

A bundle of leather armor in pale blue sat on a table, tied with a silver ribbon.

Since she couldn't remove the rings herself, yet, she might as well play along.

She stepped out some time later to find Gerard holding the reins of a tall stocky black horse.

Pausing, she reconsidered the animal. A kelpie. A magical creature who preferred water, though could travel on land.

"A now jailed trader forced this kelpie through deserts and over dry mountains. She is willing to carry you in your travels to pay your debts," Gerard petted the kelpie's head gently, "even through a sandstorm."

"What do you get out of this, kelpie?"

"I serve the greater good," a soft voice burbled, "This will enable me to see wrongs put right."

"Do you have a name you would like me to call you, kelpie?"

"Waterfall," the kelpie dropped her head.

"Then you may call me Mary," Mary took the reins from Gerard.

Mary swung up onto Waterfall, settled in the saddle as Gerard walked to the tent.

"King Gerard, why did you save me?"

He turned back, "I'm a prophet. I knew I had to be my kingdom's hero for the assault on your tower. When you brought down the barrier I saw raging fire sweeping my homeland, turning my people to ashes. I heard what you said to the grey man, and entered the room. You hung limp in the grey man's arms. He dropped you, revealing your face. I saw you in the future, queenly dressed and cooing to a baby you held, your face as it is now."

"A queen? Who would take me? Come on Waterfall, let's start our hero work."

Waterfall started down the path, when Gerard said, "That wasn't all."

She looked back, "What? I slay another dragon in that vision?"

He smiled, "What made me cut off the head of your attacker was who joined you to cradle that child."

"Who?"

He smiled, "You'll figure it out before you get to the road and have to turn either south or north."

He ducked inside the tent, dropping the flap after him.

She frowned as she faced forward again.

Waterfall had gone two steps when she whirled back around, "You have got to be kidding me. You?"

"I want at least two children," his voice replied.

She shook her head, "You are evil."

"Evil enough to protect that child who is to come. Would you do no less?"

She huffed, turned back to the road, "This is crazy."

By the time she reached the crossroads, she realized he'd given her what she wanted before the king of Mekrone cursed her.

He'd given her a horse and the ability to travel the world.

"I wonder what happens when what I want isn't what he wants," she grumbled, then asked Waterfall, "So which way should we go?"

"North gets lots of rain," Waterfall offered hopefully.

"That's as good a reason as any. North then."

She rode off, wondering what a hero with an evil side should do.

Part II
Siren's Storm

She scowled at the meager rabbit she caught without magic, nor the aid of her kelpie steed.

This task set the bar for the worst in her unending quest to remove the damn seals placed on her.

One of her ears, partially unadorned, itched daily since the seals on it vanished. The tasks started simple. Divert a flood from a village, recover a stolen heirloom, and kill a gang of highwaymen looking to cut off her hands. They liked her rings too much to stop and think why a woman wore so many they mimicked gauntlets.

She spared the starved boy who'd fallen in with them, taken him to the artesian guild where her reputation preceded her.

Admitting a tiny bit of satisfaction at how they'd instantly paid her mind and looked over the boy seriously for blacksmith membership, she smiled.

Lady Mary, Champion of the Hundred Kingdoms.

She wondered if perhaps they also knew her original title.

Siren.

Sighing, she went back to her steed, securing the rabbit in a bag.

She'd head back to deliver the rabbit to the mayor who commanded her to fetch it. Unfortunately for her, he called one of the rulers of the Hundred Kingdoms uncle, and possessed the ability to set her tasks. Ones that should she fail, she'd need to work twice as hard to remove the seal of that kingdom.

She mounted up easily unto Waterfall, and grumbled, "Back to the mayor."

"It's about to rain. Cheer up," Waterfall trumpeted before trotting back to town.

"I detest the rodent that ordered me to this menial effort. As if my powers were of no interest to him. I rather sweep aside my task, crushing waves to sand castles."

Waterfall considered, tilting her head, "We could head to the war on the outer edge. They need that sort of attitude."

Mary sulked, "He forbade that."

"Who?"

"You know who. King Gerard. The sneaky bastard. Sending an urgent missive to wander the eastern border, instead of wading into the thick of things."

"He cared to keep you free of the carnage."

"I do not," she paused, looked down to her right.

A short man stood at the edge of the trail. No, not a man. A dwarf.

"Miss," he pulled down his hat, freeing fiery red hair, "Would you be Lady Mary?"

She felt an instant of hate another quest found her, before she pushed it away, "I am. Is there a task needing my attention?"

He shook his head quickly, "Nay, milady. I am humbled to meet you. You are a godsend."

She frowned, "A godsend?"

He smiled, "Aye. Your flood uncovered new mines and deposits. My clan is in your debt."

"Hern! Where are you? The water will get cold," a larger dwarf male pushed through the bushes at the back of the first one.

"It's Lady Mary!" Hern responded.

The new dwarf looked up at her, then the kelpie, "By Gront, it is you. Please come share our fire."

She noted their ragged appearance, the lack of normal dwarf bulk. Hern looked gaunt, which she thought impossible for a dwarf.

Remembering the days she scrambled at the magicked pantry door, her body wasting away, she felt pity.

Forgetting the mayor, she dismounted Waterfall, "I will gladly join you."

She sat minutes later at the center of a boisterous group, all dwarf men. Every one of them emaciated.

The cauldron of a pot hung over the fire, quiet obviously lacking anything but water and pieces of one scraggly carrot.

She pulled down the bag with the rabbit and offered it to the dwarf who'd invited her back, "Please accept this as a contribution to the pot tonight, master dwarf."

"We could not. You are an honored guest, Lady Mary," he looked stubborn, huffing so hard his brown mustache blew up.

"A guest should offer something to share, as equally as her hosts," and they needed the meat more than her.

She recognized pride in the stance and set of his shoulders. She'd seen it often in her mirror over the years.

The eldest dwarf petted his silver beard, "Come now, Master Kral. Let us share so she may sit and enjoy our company."

Kral looked over his clan, then gave in, "I will gladly accept the offering of Lady Mary."

She sat next to the elder dwarf, "What brings you to the woods of Tharnforth? I haven't seen a mountain nor hill in half a week's ride."

He pulled out the rabbit, looked so happy she hide her smile, even as the elder dwarf harrumphed angrily.

"We lost the rights to our mine and sent seeking another by way of the boot. Damn the Holdrums and their sneaky ways."

"How would a dwarf lose their mine? You mine it, it's yours," she turned to the elder to listen better.

"There is more to it than that. Our family worked the mines for centuries so we should have owned it. However, the Holdrums snuck in while we fought goblins and mined."

She sighed, "So they created a second claim to the mine. The Lord of the Mountain would have to side with one group or the other."

"He sided with the Holdrums, rather than us loyal Stonesieges," the elder snorted, "Never did like him since his father passed away. Good dwarf that one when he left this world."

"Treachery will find its end," she knew that well.

She killed the king who cursed her to a tower and an evil path.

"Aye. Sooner the better."

"How did you Stonesieges end up so far from the mountains? Surely there are other mines to claim?"

"For a long time there were none. Then the flood came from Mekrone. We had a sizable claim then. Settled with the wives and babies for a time."

Every face drew tight with grief.

"I apologize for intruding on private grief," she said softly as Hern added the rabbit to the water.

"You saved us from death with your flood. What happened after was our own fault. The Holdrums came after us when they heard we struck rubies bigger than theirs. We argued with them and missed the shadow rats."

She knew of them. The deceased Dark Mage preferred them as his minions of terror. They could shred a body in seconds if the horde grew large enough.

"I'm sorry," she considered the flame, knowing they suffered greatly, "These Holdrums sound....evil."

Kral shook a finger at her, "I will not be the one to set free Siren. You did us a good turn that also hurt others. You must follow the light, no matter the darkness behind."

She bristled briefly, then accepted she had to stay on the path. She finally lived her childhood dream. She travelled, saw the world. Even if she collected quests the good guys seemed to live for.

"If they bother you again, let me know. They get only two free passes," she needed allies out here. Some of the rulers hated her with a vengeance.

"That is kind of you," Hern stirred the pot, "We'll find another mine."

She saw Kral's expression and knew out here finding a mine would be a miracle, assuming no humans had built on or owned the land. Their future looked bleak.

"Then I hope you find it, and you regain your happiness."

The elder spoke at length of glittering mines, the sound of rock creaking overhead, and the crack of tool on stone.

She blinked, surprised to be handed a bowl that smelled wonderful.

"Thank you," she tasted it and didn't know how to react.

"Problem?"

"No. It reminds me of my mother's cooking," she felt wetness on her cheek.

When she wiped it away, she wondered why she cried.

"You are no stranger to hardship."

She looked at Kral, confused, "I thought everyone knew the story of my fall."

"I only heard King Gerard spared you and set you on this path as a champion, instead of killed while Siren. The stories of Siren make you into a thirty foot water demoness who'd kill any man who crossed you. We shared some of our pain. Will you share yours?"

"Did you ever hear of the Dark Mage?"

They drew back, "His reputation in flaying heroes alive is well known."

"When he was defeated, I had barely seen ten years. My mother and father lived through those dark times. I was sealed by the king of Mekrone in the Dark Mage's tower. When I freed myself, my mother laid dead eight years, my father seven."

"It is your mother's cooking that drew tears," Kral shook his head, "I will never understand how evil can continue, when we have so many heroes in the world."

"Some evil is born, some made, and others ignored," she heard the hard tone and shook herself, "I wonder what I would have done if I hadn't fallen prey to the king's machinations."

"You wouldn't be Lady Mary," Hern stated firmly, "And we may have died long before this meeting without your flood."

"You remember the cave elves?" The elder chuckled, "Trying to poison us out of existence."

"Poison?" she asked.

"That is how we came to be Stonesieges. The cave elves poisoned us for centuries, killed off the weakest until we remained. We can tell when something is poison. We use to be the royal poison testers. Before the Holdrums took over with their methods."

They sent them back into cursing the Holdrum clan with bitterness. She enjoyed the meal as she memorized the names of the most devious of the Holdrum lot.

They insisted she stay the night in their camp.

She unrolled the simple durable bedroll Gerard supplied her with and laid down, pondering the brilliant field of stars overhead.

The flood which freed her from the tower prison damaged many lives. All of whom were counted on the damned jewelry she wore. Yet, she brought good into the world with the same action. The Stonesieges gained a new mine.

If she came across a mine unclaimed by dwarves or men, she'd find a way to get word back to this clan. How though? A bird? Too slow. An elemental? Hers rose from water and would cause fear rather than happiness.

Pondering on this, she fell asleep to the sounds of snores.

***

Waterfall rolled Mary out of bed the next day by grabbing a corner of the bedroll and lifting.

Grumbling at her steed and the soft wicker the kelpie gave, she dusted herself off and stood.

Light had yet to color the clouds, much less rise enough to flood the land with daybreak.

She looked over at the sleeping dwarves and wished she had some way to get them word swiftly, should she find a suitable home for them. Everyone deserved a home and children.

Shaking her head at her foolishness, she wound up her bedroll, then stowed it.

Today she'd face the stupid mayor and take her extended sentence.

Mounting Waterfall, she directed toward the road.

She arrived back at the road when the elderly dwarf appeared from beneath the ground. She smelled his magic and realized he commanded earth and stone just like King Gerard.

"Leaving without saying goodbye?" He tsked.

"I have to return to the one who set me a task I've failed. I rather do it quickly than dawdle. What of you elder?"

He tossed a black item to her.

She caught it, finding a marbled black rock in her hand.

"I won't live long and my clan needs an ally of power. That stone will convey your words and needs. If you require us, then whisper to it and set it on any ground, stone or soil. We will know of your need."

"Here I puzzled all night for naught. I thank you elder," she put it in her side pouch carefully securing the ties, "I hope our paths shall cross when your fortune has turned for the better, Elder Stonesieges."

He smiled, "At least you remember the name of the clan. Not many humans do that any more. Go on, and by Gront, may your next task be bested easily."

She nodded to him, then set Waterfall into motion again.

She glanced back once, to see the elderly dwarf limp back towards his remaining clan members.

***

The meadow to her right waved in the wind howling up on her and Waterfall half a day later.

She grumbled as she clutched her cloak in a tight fist.

Her eyes constantly swept over the grass and road, looking for signs of danger.

When something small burst out of the grass a yard in front of Waterfall, she already pulled the kelpie to a halt.

A young boy, tear streaked and panting for breathe.

His eyes landed on her hands then her adorned ear.

He collapsed with a plaintive wail, "Lady Mary, please help!"

She dismounted, came to his side, blocking the wind from his shivering body, "What is the matter? A bandit? A monster?"

"My sister. She's very ill. She...she's dying!" The boy clung to her, "Pl...please, save her."

Going back to the mayor would be pointless. However this boy needed her help now.

She picked him up, swung them both into Waterfall's saddle, "Where?"

He pointed across the grass.

"Waterfall, go!" Mary wrapped the boy in her cloak, trying to warm him with her heat.

The kelpie gave a trumpet worthy of a warhorse, then flew through the grass.

"Boy, tell me of your sister's plight. How long has she been ill?"

"A long time. The apothecary's potions slowed her sickness. She went grey this morning and she can't hardly breathe."

She spotted his home. A cottage built into a hill, utterly covered in grass and vines. The door swayed back and forth, falling apart from disrepair.

"Are your father or mother home?" She asked, "Are they sick?"

"Mama and papa went away. They haven't come back."

Waterfall clopped to a stopped, neighed.

Mary slid from the saddle, carried the boy into the cottage, his shivering getting worse.

A girl lay on a pallet, her blond hair tangled and matted. Blue tinge creeped in on her lips as she rasped in each breath.

"Let my brother down!"

Mary dodged the cudgel swung at her, clutching the boy so she didn't drop him.

The young man snarled, readied to swing again.

"I am Lady Mary," she stated calmly, her eyes on the man.

"Prove it!" the man snapped.

She raised an eyebrow, then looked out the door, "Waterfall, you want to introduce yourself?"

Waterfall looked around the door frame, "Good day. I'm Waterfall."

The young man dropped his weapon, staring at the kelpie.

Mary noticed the hearth lay cold. No fire burned.

It fit with the cold temperature inside the cottage.

"Do you have firewood?"

The man blinked as he stared at her.

"Firewood for the hearth. Your brother needs warmth," she set the boy down in front of the hearth, taking off her cloak to blanket him.

"It's all wet," he sounded young.

"Good thing I have an affinity with water. Go on. I'll start tending to your sister," she knelt beside the girl, touching her forehead.

"Why is the great Lady Mary helping us? God forsook us."

"You wouldn't believe my tale if I told it. Get the fire wood so we can warm your siblings. Waterfall, escort him."

"Yes, my lady," Waterfall nipped his shirt, tugged him after her.

"Will you save my sister?"

She looked at the shivering boy, his wide blue eyes, "I will do my best. I will be in deep focus. Will you listen for danger? If you shout, I will hear and wake."

He nodded, his face going grave as he faced the open door.

She turned back to her charge, and slipped into the healer's focus. She'd done it often for her wounded creatures so she sank into her magic easily.

Sending her mind into the girl's body, she raced through, observing the damage, starting with her blood.

That is where she found the poison. Being water based, Mary recognized it immediately.

A stream fish produced this particular poison as a defense from its enemies. The fish came from her former kingdom.

She knew it would be delicate, so she began the spell to purge the girl. Mary summoned her water elemental in its smallest form and carefully directed it to collect the poison, isolating it from the girl.

When Mary finished she shook as badly as the boy.

She eased back, wiped her forehead, soaking her sleeve with sweat.

"She's getting better," the man said in awe.

"I was in time," Mary looked up at the man, "The firewood?"

He pointed to a stack so waterlogged it oozed unto the floor.

She stood, swaying slightly before moving forward.

She sat wearily next to the wood, cross legged. This spell would be easier. Her water elemental absorbed water from the ponds, soil, even the air.

She sent it to suck up the water from the logs, watching it carefully.

When it finished she let it go to rest, ending the spell.

Picking up one of the bone dry logs she set it in the hearth.

"I'll get the fire started," the man moved swiftly.

The boy crawled into her lap. She wrapped the cloak around them both.

She watched the man get tinder to catch, and welcomed the blaze he coaxed easily.

"Does your sister," she started, "go to a particular stream or river nearby? To perhaps wash the clothes?"

The man scowled, "She bathes upstream of where we do, near a basin. She washes our clothes downstream of where we bath. Don't know where."

"I do."

Mary looked down into the boy's earnest face, "Which one?"

"Both. I help her with laundry and look out."

Hence why he took the order to guard so seriously. He did it with his sister.

"When I have recovered, I will need you to guide me. The poison is from a fish. I need to find out where she met the fiend to confirm it."

"A fish? We eat fish from the streams often."

"This is a fish not native to your land. It's from Mekrone, my home."

Inside she feared she brought this fish here. Her flood must have unleashed the poisonous scoundrel into this kingdom. How many more lives had she destroyed by breaching the tower?

"Samuel?" A weak voice asked.

The man rushed to the girl, "Talia, I'm here sister."

"Make sure Mathias practices tying knots. He wants to fish soon."

Mary looked at Talia's fever-bright eyes and knew she saw something different.

"Tell mama and papa to bring home some vegetables," Talia smiled and then fell asleep.

Samuel's face told her why Mathias thought his parents gone away and the cottage decayed. Their mother and father had died.

"Samuel, Waterfall has a skein of pure water. Get her to drink some. I will need my bedroll as well, if you would get it too."

He nodded, "Yes...my lady."

Mathias looked up at her, then snuggled closer to her.

She stared into the fire, her mind going blank.

"Here, my lady. Your bed is ready," Samuel stated, shaking her.

She blinked at him, then the bedroll beside her, ready for sleep.

Stiffly she crawled onto the roll, laid down with Mathias still clinging to her.

***

She woke to Waterfall nibbling her ear.

"Can we go find the fish? I can play in the stream while we look for it."

Mary gave Waterfall a dark look, "You just want to roll in the water while I do all the hard work."

"That too," Waterfall unashamedly replied.

"Kelpies," Mary grumbled sitting up.

Samuel sat propped against the wall, fast asleep. Mathias lay beside him, curled up in a blanket. Talia looked better than last night, her skin losing the unhealthy pallor.

Mary stood, cracking her back.

"So what fish are we looking for?"

She gave Waterfall an arched glance, "It's called Malrir. It's responsible for hundreds of deaths each year. They range in color and pattern as they blend into their surroundings. They tend to be vicious and territorial. It's possible Talia encountered them at the stream."

"So we go play now with the Malrir?"

"Only you would think of dancing with Malrir as if they were friends."

Mary walked out into open, noting the dawn light bursting over the distant tree line.

"You should have breakfast," Waterfall nipped Mary's shirt, preventing Mary from walking away.

"Very well," Mary pulled out a length of jerky, chewed on it as she considered the land.

Someone would certainly want to claim it. Forest nearby with animals and wood. Nearby water source. If someone cleared the grass, the ground could bear grains of one sort or another.

Why hadn't anyone come to kick the children out?

"Why are you frowning?" Samuel asked, joining her, his face hard.

"This is good land. Have you been approached by the locals to sell it?"

He snorted, "Many times since the folks went off and met their maker. I want to sell and go out into the world, but Talia won't have none of it."

"Your parents owned this land without debt?"

"One of our distant ancestors did a huge service to the king. He granted this land to our family so we would prosper."

Like the dwarves had staked their claim then lost it, these children would lose their ancestral home. Partly due to disinterest.

"So Talia is the one who wants to stay," Mary looked over the land, "With a good man, she could make it work."

Samuel huffed before storming inside.

Waterfall asked softly, "Why would that upset him?"

Sighing, Mary looked into the cottage, "He thinks he is being punished for abandoning his home and now he is not a good man."

"Not a problem. Go find new home."

"It's not so simple as that. He views it as disloyalty to his family. The last of his family," she strode inside the cottage.

Mathias yawned as he stood up, rubbing his eyes with his fists.

"Are you feeling well, Mathias?" She asked gently.

"Yes!" He jumped up and down, "Can we go now?"

"Eat something first," Mary said, ignoring the snicker of Waterfall.

She turned to Samuel, "Would you watch over Talia while I confirm the poison's source and deal with it?"

He looked at Talia, "Will she get better?"

"She'll need time and to avoid a second poisoning. I'll see if I can lend her some of my strength to speed her recovery once I've removed the problem."

"I'll watch her. Just fix this."

She smiled, "Yes, milord."

Samuel looked appalled as Mary walked out to Waterfall.

"Are we going to the stream now?" Mathias looked up at her as he came to her side.

"Yes. I would like to see the laundry location first, then your bathing area, then Talia's."

"You think the fish is at the laundry spot?" Mathias jumped up into her arms, clinging to her.

She swung up onto Waterfall, settled them both, "I don't know. I need to find it to confirm the source."

She looked at Samuel, then pulled a horn from her saddlebag, "If you need me, sound this. I'll return."

He grimaced, but accepted, "I will," he hesitated, "Please keep Mathias safe."

She nodded, then nudged Waterfall into a trot towards the tree line.

***

She touched the water at the laundry spot, noting she could see the bottom easily. She sent out a pulse through the water, sensing the fish around her.

Nothing even close to the Malrir.

Mathias giggled, making her look at him as he petted Waterfall's leg.

"You look funny."

She smiled at his innocence, "Magic can seem like that, but you should be careful. Wizards are quick to transform those who offend," she looked over the stream, "I cast out to see what fish live here. None are poisonous. These are safe to eat."

Straightening, she pondered the opposite bank. The trees swayed without wind.

"Announce yourselves," she demanded, readying to summon her elemental.

A tiny creature peeked around the tree, eyes wide and yellow in a face of brown fur. It had four arms, each loaded with branches.

She blinked, "A tree keeper."

It stared at her a long moment, then vanished.

"Did that hurt my sister?" Mathias asked in a quiet voice.

"No. They are a good omen. It means the trees here are healthy and well tended. Less chance of wild fire," she went to the boy, knelt, "If you treat his trees well, he may leave downed branches at your door."

"You looked scary," he hid behind Waterfall.

"I thought bandits were hiding out there. I didn't want you hurt."

"I'm sorry. I don't want you to die for me."

He started crying.

She rubbed his back, helpless against his tears.

"Why do you think I'll die?"

"Flightwind, our guardian died guarding me."

"Why don't you tell me about Flightwind while we head to your bathing area," she picked him up, put him in the the saddle before joining him.

Waterfall sauntered upstream.

"He was a huge hawk. My mother trained him before she left. She said he'd guard us until she got back. He took an arrow for me while I guarded my sister."

Mary felt a frisson of alarm, "Did a hunter mistake you?"

"We never found who fired it. Flightwind was my friend. He caught rabbits for our soups."

Mathias pointed at an open spot, "Samuel and I use this place."

She dismounted, but held up a hand to Mathias, "Stay on Waterfall. Waterfall, stand there," she indicated the only area that she could stand and be hidden from most directions, "I don't think this is the spot since it was your sister poisoned, Mathias."

His eyes got wide, "We are healthy so not here?"

She nodded proudly, "Exactly. Logic is a good skill to nurture."

Waterfall whined, "I want to play in the water."

Mary tapped Waterfall on the nose reproachfully, "Stay, girl."

The spell confirmed this spot didn't have Malrir either. The water flowed, slight muddy. Malrir didn't like murky water. Their blending ability didn't work so well in dirty water.

She returned to her companions, "No Malrir. Let's find Talia's bathing spot."

"We'll have to circle around," Mathias sighed, "It'll take ten minutes at least."

Mary mounted up, considered the water that spilled downstream.

"Waterfall, over the water, not in it," she ordered firmly.

"Water?" Waterfall leapt over to the middle of the stream.

She landed lightly on the water, splashing happily.

Mathias looked down in awe, "She's walking on water."

"Better than in it," Mary grumbled, remembering Waterfall racing through an ocean. Luckily, her elemental could form a bubble and protect the occupant, "Upstream."

Waterfall neighed happily and raced up the stream.

The water grew steadily muddier, almost black.

"Is the water normally this dark, Mathias?"

"No. It's clear."

They came to the spot Talia bathed at within a couple minutes.

Only two openings: one to the river and the pool she used to bath, and the way into the woods.

Mary reined in Waterfall, realizing anyone firing an arrow at the river would see clearly who they shot at.

A murder attempt?

The water swirled slowly by as she dismounted to check the water.

Her spell said there were no Malrir, but other fish skulked in the murk. Again, none that produced poison.

"No Malrir, however, I want to know what is causing the water to be so silty. It may have driven the Malrir downstream," she mounted again, turned Waterfall upstream.

"You think it's intentional?" Waterfall asked as she trotted over stones and water.

"Too recent to be otherwise."

***

An hour later they turned around a wall of rocks, to see a splash rise up a good twenty feet into the air.

The water in the distance looked clear until it reached this point.

"Waterfall, get close to that boulder, then pull back after I'm on it," Mary looked up but saw no rocks that accounted for the splash.

Mary dismounted unto the submerged boulder, water eddying around her boots, "Mathias, stay with Waterfall. If this is the Malrir, I don't want you poisoned too."

"You think the Malrir are here?"

"Something is here," she saw his blank look, "The water is clearing, so something caused the splashing. Perhaps falling rocks," she pointed up the cliff, "So stay back."

Waterfall pulled back around the rock wall, cheerfully stated, "When we are done here, we can run in the water."

"We are not running in the water," Mary stated firmly.

"Awww," Mathias whined.

Kneeling, Mary set her hand on the muddy water and sent out her spell.

No fish, but she sensed a water spirit.

A large healthy one.

"Honored one of the stream. I seek your wisdom in matters of your stream."

It whispered to her through the water, "You speak politely for one who controls such a water elemental."

Mary nodded, "I do not wish a fight with you, honored one. I seek knowledge of the Malrir."

"What are Malrir?"

"They are a fish poisonous to humans. The daughter of the landowners was stricken with their poison. I healed her and now wish to find the source to prevent more harm."

The water spirit popped out of the water, it's face right in Mary's. It looked vaguely like an otter, just transparent blue. The water around it cleared of the mud.

"Talia is sick?"

Mary spoke softy, "Yes, honored one. I cured her of the poison, but she must recover. Have you seen the Malrir that harmed her?"

It hissed showing sharp teeth that would do a dire wolf proud, "I do not stand poison fish in my stream. When the flood brought some here, I killed them then washed their bodies over the bank."

"I am grateful for this wisdom, honored one," she pause on a thought since this spirit knew about Talia, "I have brought Talia's brother with me. Would you allow him to see you, honored one?"

"Only if you do me a boon in return."

Mary mentally sighed. It seemed she collected quests. Being a champion required a lot of work.

"What may I do for you, honored one?"

"I will tell you when Talia's brother is here."

The water spirit vanished into the water.

Mary stood, then called for Waterfall.

She trotted up, Mathias looking around curiously.

"Mathias, I would like to introduce you to someone," Mary reached out and held onto Waterfall's halter.

She turned and bowed briefly to the water spirit she could see in the clear water, "This is the spirit of the stream. Honored one, this is Mathias, brother to Talia."

The spirit's head rose out of the water, turned its head so it could look at Mathias.

Mathias bowed his head, almost unseating himself. Mary caught him around his waist, steading him.

The spirit burbled happily, "You bathe downstream of Talia with the bigger one. You like swimming with the fish."

"Yes. It's fun. They tickle."

The spirit appeared pleased with his answer, "Continue to treat my stream well and you will have clean water."

"Okay," he promised with a big smile.

The spirit turned to Mary, "I need your help to keep the bad rock from my water."

"Bad rock?" Mary made sure Mathias sat firmly in the saddle before kneeling, "Where is the bad rock?"

The spirit pointed its nose up the cliff, "That white rock. It will hurt my magic if it drops in my stream."

Mary looked up the cliff, spotted the tiny white rock among the wet soil. The water spirit must have been trying to wash the rock up over the cliff.

"I'll need to use my water elemental to get to it. Will you allow me to?" Mary asked the spirit.

It nodded, then splashed into the water.

"Waterfall keep an eye on Mathias. Mathias I need to focus on my magic. Please sit quietly."

He looked stern again, eyes scanning the cliffs.

Mary stepped onto the water, her water elemental supporting her, before it carried her to the bottom of the cliff. Then it lifted her up twenty feet to the white rock. She touched it, a shock jolting her.

She pulled the stone free, recognizing it despite the white color. It normally would be red if it had been charged by ley lines.

In her palm rested a depleted leystone. Any Mage with money would give it all away to own a finger nail sized stone. The one she held filled her palm.

The reason for such a pale color was it came from a larger lode. One with at least hundred stones of the same size together.

She made her elemental raise her above the cliff.

Scanning the ground she spotted signs that the lode lay a great distance inland.

Only dwarves could mine a lode of leystones safely.

She directed her elemental to return her to Waterfall as she set the leystone into her pouch.

"I have collected the bad rock. I will pursue options to prevent others from coming to your stream, honored one," she said to the water as she swung onto Waterfall.

The spirit did not respond.

"Waterfall. Let's return to the cottage."

"What is that stone?" Mathias asked.

"I need to speak to you all. What did you think of who you met today?"

"I wondered who Talia spoke to. She also talked to Flightwind like that."

An animal speaker? Mary wondered who their parents had been.

***

A little over an hour later they arrived back to the cottage.

A cloaked man crossed the grass to the road, his body language distraught as he walked briskly away. Mary scowled after him a moment, something about his manner teasing her with oddities.

Dismissing him for the time being, she rode to the cottage.

She dismounted then helped Mathias down. He raced inside the cottage, excitedly reciting what happened, the voices of Talia and Samuel alleviating Mary's concern. Why had the man leaving behaved the way he did? Talia would mend.

Shaking her head, Mary pulled out the leystone, setting it in the grass next to the cottage, hidden from sight. The ley lines would charge the stone as they should.

Straightening, she reached into her pouch for the dwarven stone.

These children couldn't mine the leystones, and the dwarves needed a mine. She could get them both to work together and be stronger than apart.

She whispered to the stone, "Come to me. I am in need of your expertise and knowledge."

Setting the stone on the ground, she watched it sink out of sight.

"Waterfall, we'll need to go into town tomorrow. We will be getting supplies."

"Supplies for what?"

Mary smiled, "Listen and you'll figure it out. Don't touch that stone. It could hurt you."

She stepped inside closing the door as best she could.

Talia smiled up at her, "You are the champion?"

Mary nodded, "Lady Mary. You are recovering from poison."

She sighed, "From a fish?"

Mary sat on the floor, Samuel handing her a bowl of soup, "Malrir is the name of the fish. I spoke with the spirit in the stream and confirmed the fish did not come from there."

"You also saw the tree keeper. They don't come out to strangers often," Talia smiled.

"I nearly attacked the tree keeper before I knew what he was. You have two blessings for this land already."

"Father showed me the tree keeper. I discovered the stream spirit on my own."

Mary continued, "I made another discovery. The stream spirit was upset about a stone. The stone I took from the wall of the cliff is a leystone."

Talia stared at her in surprise as Samuel blinked.

"There are no more leystones," Samuel stated firmly.

Mary went outside, retrieved the stone and came back.

She handed it to him, "It's pale as it had others of its size around it. It couldn't get fully charged and turn the signature red it is known for. The water spirit didn't want it taking energy from the stream. Dwarves are the only ones who can mine and cut them."

"It would take weeks before a scout could get here," Samuel gave her the stone back, "Then we would have to wait until part of a clan would arrive."

"It so happens there is a clan a couple days out, looking for a mine to call their own. If you want I can broker a deal between you as the owners of the land and them. If the lode is as big as I think, you could hire helpers for the farming and tending of the cottage while allowing you to find your paths."

Talia smiled, "Mother said a great secret lay in the land only dwarves could uncover. We'll get plenty of money. Samuel, you can go out and travel," she patted his knee weakly, "I can stay and tend the land while Mathias grows."

"How can we call these dwarves? A messenger?"

"I sent a message already. I will go into town and get supplies so you do not need to worry about your guests once they arrive."

She stood, walked outside and set the stone back on the ground.

Looking at the fields she wondered if she could avoid the mayor, since she failed his stupid quest, long enough to do some good here.

Waterfall asked, "Why can't I play with the stone?"

"It draws magic from ley lines. You are made more of magic than I, so it could absorb you. Stay clear. I need your help tomorrow with the supplies and you can't be drained."

"The stone is that important?"

"A fingernail sized one can empower a lesser magus to control an elemental like mine. Someone like me uses them to enhance our abilities and sustain large spells. It could allow me to control elementals that are not water for a few seconds."

She did not relish the thought of trying. Her last attempt to control fire, earth and wind scarred her. A healer lessened the scars but she didn't want to incur them again.

"It is very valuable as it's the size of my hoof?"

Mary looked up at Waterfall, whispered, "Yes. Very valuable. Once the dwarves assess the lode I'll know how likely the poison and the death of Flightwind is related."

Waterfall looked at the cottage, "You think evil is a hoof?"

"We'll see. Keep watch. Tomorrow will be interesting."

Mary stepped inside, then asked, "The cloaked man I saw leaving your field. Is he a friend?"

"A family friend. He was concerned when my brothers didn't come to pick up the medicine," Talia smiled, "He's kindly helped us since our folks left."

Mary nodded, but something still bothered her. Talia was on the mend, so why show almost grief stricken posture?

A question for later.

***

Mary stretched the next morning, planning how to spread the news her quest had gotten interesting.

Just not the quest the mayor gave her.

"Samuel," she got up and then shook him.

He blearily opened his eyes as he looked at Talia.

"I will be going to town and get the supplies for the dwarves. Will you be alright by yourselves?"

"I can defend my family," he growled as he stood up proudly.

"Good. Here," she held out a pouch, "This has some dried meats and vegetables. You can see if Talia will eat."

He took it, "We need firewood."

Mary opened the door, then blinked at the pile of the branches laying across the doorway.

"It seems we made an impression on the tree keeper," she looked back to see Mathias' wide eyes, "He left some firewood for you."

She stepped over the pile, collected the stone, noting it approached a rosy color, before securing it in a pouch.

Waterfall trotted up, carrying a bucket of water, "Ah goff dis doff em."

Mary took the bucket and asked, "What was that Waterfall?"

"I got that for them. The stream spirit played with me, too."

Rolling her eyes, Mary set the bucket inside the cottage, "Of course you did. Enough play. We have work to do to prepare for the dwarves."

"Yes. Town and supplies!" Waterfall danced in place joyfully.

Mary mounted up, looked down at Mathias who looked at the branches in awe.

"Mathias, you make sure to keep an eye on Talia. I look forward to your report on my return."

"Visit the apothecary," Samuel ordered from the hearth, "We purchased more of Talia's medicine."

Mary bowed sarcastically, making Mathias giggle, "Of course, milord."

Before Samuel could respond, she sent Waterfall towards town.

She wondered when he purchased more medicine. She'd ask upon her return.

When she rode into town an hour later, she went to the village supplier first.

Dismounting, Mary walked into the shop.

"Why Lady Mary. What may I help you with today?" The proprietor smiled.

"How much would you recommend to feed a dwarf for a single day?"

"Well a healthy dwarf needs about half a barrel of food a day," he petted his beard, "Would you be looking for provisions for several days?"

"A week for ten dwarves," she watched his face go blank, "I'll be back with a wagon to pick it up," she fished out half the price, "I'll pay the rest on my return. Would you also be able to recommend a place I could acquire a wagon and ale?"

"Of course. The blacksmith at the other end of town crafts some fine wagons. The tavern, Golden Spiral, has good ale, but there is also the ale makers near the blacksmith. Their ale use to be preferred by the dwarves when they use to be here."

"Use to be here?" Mary asked.

"We were the center of the ley stone mining region. When the mines played out, the dwarves left. Why are there dwarves here now?"

She smiled, "That is part of a quest I am on. I want them well fed and happy so I can complete it. I'll be back for the provisions."

By the time she found the blacksmith, word had spread she hosted dwarves.

The blacksmith stood beside a sizable wagon, waiting for her with a decent price. He also asked if a new mine had been opened. She replied she needed dwarven expertise on her quest. She did not know if a new mine had been found or not.

She harnessed Waterfall to the wagon and walked with her to the ale makers, who waited for her outside their warehouse.

She purchased three kegs at their urging before walking down to the apothecary.

Mary walked into his store, the overwhelming scent of lavender irritating her nose.

"Lady Mary," the apothecary smiled nervously at her, "what brings you to my humble shop?"

"At request of Samuel, I am here to pick up Talia's medicine," she looked around, seeing he kept well stocked with common components for mages and wizards.

She walked over to a jar of Harleter root. It formed the basis of most non-elemental spells.

"How much for a piece of Harleter?" She turned back to him.

He hadn't moved.

"Is something wrong?" She faced him.

"I just don't see someone of your fame running an errand for a couple of children," he laughed nervously as he turned and pulled down a bottle, "Here is Talia's supply of medicine. Harleter is out of season, so I'll have to charge you a gold."

"I'll skip the Harleter," she picked up the bottle, "Perhaps later. I'll deliver this to Talia. Have a good day, apothecary."

She returned to the provisioner and collected her barrels, paying him the remaining cost.

Ensuring straps kept the load from shifting, she started back to the cottage.

Walking with Waterfall, she noted everyone watched her, chatting hurriedly. Most sounded hopeful, and said "Dwarves," often.

"You encouraged the whole village with curiosity."

Mary glanced at Waterfall, "I merely said the truth, with a hint of implication dwarves are helping me with my quest."

"The mayor won't like that."

"I don't care. That quest was beneath me. Helping Mathias, Samuel, Talia and the Stonesieges clan, that is my level."

"You could ride the cart. It's not as heavy as some I've pulled," Waterfall offered an hour later.

Mary shook her head, "We have a while to go and you need to save strength. That family needs both of us, and the dwarves need to recover their fortitude."

She didn't admit walking allowed her to think, to focus on her options, and to tend her magics.

For the last few weeks she'd neglected some of her more hardy spells. She tended them now, ensuring they'd be available for her defense.

"We can unload soon!" Waterfall pranced ahead, making Mary look up to the cottage through the long grass.

"You just want to go play with the stream spirit again," Mary chided.

"After unloading, yes!"

Mary trotted to keep up with Waterfall as Samuel came outside, his face surprised when he saw the wagon.

"I bought a week's worth of food for the dwarves, and some ale to be shared."

"Ale?" Mathias peered around Samuel.

"You are too young," Samuel looked like he wanted to partake of the ale himself.

"Let's get this inside," Mary looked to the sky feeling something off.

"Rain!" Waterfall cheered as a flash of lightning crossed the heavens.

Mary knew it wasn't natural. Most weather mages knew not to summon a storm and release it on the world. It invited criminals to steal the magics. This storm felt like it'd been loosed by a careless yet powerful mage. Plenty of magic remained and would bring thieves down on the town in the next day or two if not corrected. She'd have to track down the mage and make him or her fix it. Yet another quest on her plate.

She got into the wagon, moving fast, "Milord, let's get these inside quickly. The storm rushes our way."

They muscled the last barrels inside as the rain slammed them.

Mary braved it to unhitched Waterfall, and let her off to play.

Soaking wet, she returned to the cottage's warmth.

The roof leaked water. She sighed, then reached out to plug the holes with her magic.

Intending to use her water elemental to freeze the holes solid, she nearly didn't catch the earth elemental who attempted to bury the cottage in mud.

She fought it so it only coated the roof, then dried into a hard clay.

The earth elemental retreated without hurting her, nor draining her of her energy.

Talia said in by soft voice, "You turned aside an earth elemental?"

Mary looked at Talia's clear eyes, saw the magic Talia wielded herself. Talia was a green warden.

A green warden guided nature through soft spells, like turning aside a flood by starting with a handful of sand.

Mary saw Talia knew someone hunted her family.

"Someone of great power sent it here to crush this cottage. I am surprise I could turn it aside."

Mathias asked, "What about the stone?"

She dug out the ley stone, noting it's diminished pale pink color.

"This is why people pay fortunes to obtain these stones," she looked at Samuel, "They can be a tool for evil."

"If you hadn't been here, we'd be dead," Talia sat up, "I am grateful to the gods you came into our lives."

Mary sat, gently using her water elemental to suck the rain off her clothes, "I hope the dwarves are here tomorrow. The faster they come, the faster we can determine the lode and if it can be mined."

"And who is trying to kill us," Talia looked to the door that screeched in the wind before it settled back into the frame, "Mathias, Flightwind sensed danger to you. That is why he took the arrow. Mother and father...they are gone, killed by bandits on the road."

Mathias teared up before he turned and burrowed against Mary.

Samuel snarled, "It would explain why that horse threw Patrick when that beast didn't spook in either Troll War."

"Patrick?" Mary asked as she rubbed Mathias' back.

"Our oldest brother. He died before mother and father," Talia coughed lightly, "Then I'm poisoned. It's too much bad fortune to be anything but intentional."

"How long has this threat hung over your family?"

"Three years?" Samuel scratched his head, sighing, "I avoided an attempt since my magic manifests as good luck against enemies."

"Mathias?" Mary got him to look up at her, "Do you have magic?"

He looked so sad, "I don't have magic."

"You are young still. Some don't get their magic until they are grown men. I imagine you'll have a wonderful ability."

He cheered up, "What do you think it will be?"

"I can't see the future. If I did, I would ride against your enemy right now," she ruffled his hair.

"You'll make them pay for those they took?"

"Yeah. They'll pay," one way or another.

Mary set the leystone near the door to soak up magic again.

They retired to bed once Waterfall returned from her romp, singing happily.

***

Mary woke before dawn and got up.

She picked up the red stone on her way out the door into the rain sweet air. She pouched the stone.

Waterfall danced about happily, splashing from one puddle to another.

Watching her companion frolic like a youngster, Mary pondered who the enemy of the children could be.

"Hail!" A happy voice boomed she instantly recognized.

"You made excellent time, Stonesieges clan," she met them halfway across the field, "please come inside. I think a meal to discuss what I found and what you can do will aid everyone involved."

Kral raised an eyebrow as his clan spread out behind him, "Indeed?"

"Dwarves!" Mathias squealed from behind Mary.

She turned to see Samuel with him, both staring at the dwarves in awe and admiration.

"This is my good friend Kral of the Stonesieges clan. Let's adjourn inside so Talia may be introduced."

Samuel and Mathias ducked inside, letting Kral enter next.

When they all sat or stood inside, a bowl of dried food to snack on, Mary related her tale so far.

When she got to the leystone Kral's eyes glistened in hope.

"May I see the stone you have used?"

She pulled it out, handed it to him.

He smiled, "This is a leystone. A good sized one. Elder, would you do the honor of cutting it?"

The elderly dwarf reverently took the stone and sat back to begin his work using tiny tools.

"I want to go see where you think the lode is. We can tell a lot about it once we see the area."

"Since we'll be about, how about some of your men stay here to guard Talia and Mathias. Milord will you be joining us?"

Samuel scowled at her, "I'm no lord but I will accompany you."

"Kral, do you feel up for a bit of a walk?"

He finished his meal, "I am."

Mary, Waterfall, Samuel, Kral and two other dwarves of his clan took off in search of the lode.

Waterfall lead them through a shortcut to the top of the cliff Mary recovered the stone from.

Kral brushed the ground, then pointed away from the stream, "This way."

They trudged for an hour to a clearing.

It showed signs of being dug up. Mary knelt near a hole, pulling back the damaged soil and grass.

Solid stone stretched under the roots, unmarred except for a single narrow hollow.

Kral knelt with her, "Tiny pieces from the lode were taken from here. My men are digging down about a foot to see if we can pull up the first stone."

"Someone else knew of this," Mary looked over the other disturbed sections, "All slivers?"

"Yes. Enough to aid a lesser man or woman to control an elemental easily with known spells," Kral stood returned to his working men.

"That means the earth elemental last night wasn't a coincidence," Samuel whispered.

She turned to Samuel, then nodded, "Word spread quickly I would have dwarven company soon. The scoundrel digging here might be behind it. This is still your land, is it not, milord?"

"The land of my family, yes. There's a deer trail beyond those trees," he pointed, "Someone could easily bring a horse up here with gear to mine. No one else lives for miles."

Kral came up and handed Samuel three stones, all white, "That is from digging for half an hour. This would keep you and your family in wealth for your lives and perhaps your children's."

Samuel asked, "The lode?"

"If it mirrors these stones," Kral grinned, "Enough to keep both our clans wealthy for hundreds of generations."

"I think we should get back and see about an agreement between the land owners and the miners," Mary started back to the cottage, "I think this will solve many ills."

They returned to a hearty stew and ale.

Mary negotiated a treaty between the children and the Stonesieges. The Stonesieges would act as wardens for the children's fortune until Samuel became fully a man in return for getting half the profits from mining the lode. The children would get the other half, spilt between them, to hire helpers and allow them to pursue their dreams.

Mary acted as scribe and produced three copies of the treaty. One to each group and one that would be filed with the king's court.

"Let's eat."

"Lady Mary, Talia needs her medicine," Samuel said as he signed the copies, passing them to Kral.

Mary retrieved the bottle from her saddlebags and held it out to Talia.

Only the Elder snatched it from her hand, "Poison."

Mary blinked at him, "Poison?"

"I could feel it nearby, but not its source. This is poison."

Mary used her magic and felt the response of Malrir poison coming from within the bottle.

"Talia, did you get worse while on this medicine?"Moshe asked the girl.

She nodded, pulling back from the group, "Yes."

Rage boiled in Mary.

The apothecary.

"Lady Mary?" Kral asked in concern.

"The apothecary. That is why he acted so nervous when I picked up Talia's medicine from him. He thought I found him out."

"He is the richest one in town besides the mayor," Samuel growled.

"He knew I wanted to keep the land," Talia sobbed, "I told him I wanted to get stronger so I could tend it like mother and father. He brought the medicine, the poison every week."

Mathias shrank in on himself.

"Mathias?" Mary put a hand on his shoulder, "What is it?"

"I told him where I saw Heathflowers. They grow right next to sister's bathing spot," he looked up, tears streaming down his face, "I killed Flightwind."

"No. He did," Mary stood, went to the door, "Waterfall!"

She ran into view, her eyes narrow, searching for danger, "Something wrong?"

Mary shouldered the saddle and saddlebags, "We are going to take the treaty to the King. That way the apothecary can't get this land ever."

While she readied Waterfall for a long trip, she tried to think of some plan to force the man into the open and take him down.

Killing three people and attempting murder on three children. To take their dreams away. She wouldn't let him do it again.

"Here, Lady Mary," the Elder called her attention.

He held out a cut sparkling gem.

She took it, hardly recognizing the leystone.

"A cut leystone is always more powerful than a raw one. Do not let it fall into evil hands."

She pouched the stone, looking at him, "I will get them justice."

"Justice for whom?" The elder gave her another summoning rock, then walked back inside.

"What did he mean?" Waterfall asked.

Shaking her head, Mary ducked into the cottage again, "Are all three copies signed?"

Mathias held out a sealed messenger tube, "Yes! Here's yours."

She took it, ruffling Mathias hair, "I'm off then. Kral, Samuel keep your families safe."

"Thank you," Talia sniffed, "You have given us back our future."

Like no one did for Mary when she'd been trapped in a tower, alone, scared and hopeless.

Shouldering the messenger tube, she looked over all of them, "If this goes right, you will no longer be bothered and may choose your path."

"If not?" Mathias looked up at her with worry.

"I am a champion, Mathias. I stand between those who can't defend themselves, and those who attack them. If today I die, then your enemy will be escorting me and will not trouble you again."

She strode out, leapt into the saddle and turned to town, "Waterfall, let's go visit the mayor on the way out."

"Why would you need to visit the mayor?" Samuel called from the doorway.

"Because he told me to catch a rabbit without magic nor aid from Waterfall. I might as well take my punishment before riding for the king's court," she laughed.

Waterfall shot off, thundering towards town.

Mary's anger returned, bubbling into her eyes.

The man attempted to kill children to get at a lode he had no right to. Like the former king of Melkrone, he sacrificed the future for glory today, damn the innocents he buried.

Waterfall shrieked in alarm as wind threw them both into the air, an elemental flinging them about.

Then Mary slammed into the ground, coughing at the dust blinding her.

"You just had to ruin everything, Siren."

Mary pushed to her feet, her teeth bared at the apothecary, "So you reveal yourself, murderer."

"I had it made. I'm respected in the village. No one would assume I killed the brat's parents nor brother. They wouldn't think I'd try to kill the brats and get the land for a pittance. You," he pointed a finger at her, the necklace of glowing red stones around his neck drawing her attention, "Siren, ruined it all. You're a villainess. Hand over the treaty you carry."

He wore a hundred tiny slivers of leystones.

It made his power her better.

She straightened, glaring regally down her nose at him, "You want Siren, then you shall have Siren!"

Her water elemental burst out of the ground in a massive wall.

"Ha. You think I didn't prepare for this?"

Pain lashed her as her elemental disappeared into a jar.

He shoved a cork into the top, "So I defeat the great Siren."

She reached up into the sky where magic from the storm swirled.

Drawing it down into herself, she summoned an air elemental to her side.

The man gaped at the lightning beast in front of him.

"Kill him!" Mary snarled.

The apothecary screamed, trying to fight her for control of the air elemental.

She heard something thud behind her but she refused to break her focus.

The stones stopped glowing on his necklace and he went flying from a crackling bolt.

Waterfall suddenly stood between the air elemental and the downed apothecary.

"Get out of the way, Waterfall," Mary hissed.

"No! You have to bring him to justice. He is defeated. He must answer for his crimes by trail."

"He must die. He cannot be allowed to hurt another child."

Waterfall stared at her for a long moment then replied softly, "Is that Siren, the foul villainess who slays her enemies without mercy, or is it Mary who deserves happiness at the end of her quests?"

Mary heard Gerard's voice, saying she would hold a baby, and have him by her side.

A champion wouldn't do this.

She released the air elemental back to the storm, letting it collect the magic to disperse naturally. At least she wouldn't have to make the mage fix it now she dealt with it.

Waterfall lowered her head, "Are you going to kill him?"

"Not right now," she walked over to him, snatching the jug from his limp fingers.

Her elemental returned to her once the seal broke.

She ordered her elemental to encase the apothecary in a bubble, floating him off the ground with enough air for him to live.

"Let's give this...criminal to the mayor. He looks like a rabbit. Just as cowardly as his smaller brethren."

Mary swung up onto Waterfall and they continued into town.

The townspeople scurried out of their way, eyes frightened. Mary knew she looked like she'd been in a fight.

She turned the corner to head toward the mayor's estate, when she noticed a fancy carriage sitting in the street.

Ten guards came to attention, another running inside.

Waterfall came to a stop before the guards, letting Mary look over the carriage's symbol.

It looked familiar. She couldn't recall from where.

"Why Lady Mary!"

She turned and looked at the gold and white robed man.

The king.

He paused between his guards as the mayor came running out.

She dismounted, making sure she didn't release the criminal.

"I request a private audience with your excellency and the mayor," she looked at the mayor coldly, "There are many matters in need of discussion."

"My healer will see to your wounds," The king swept inside.

"He may need to see to the wounds of my prisoner," she walked after him, the bubble bobbing behind her.

She stood before the king as he sat in the audience room, the mayor behind him.

Telling her adventure with the children, the dwarves and the new mine, she calmed down. She waited to tell of the apothecary's crimes.

"I bring the treaty between the landlords of a new leystone mine, and the Stonesieges clan from the dwarven region," she finished that part of her tale, handing over the tube to one of his guards.

The king took the messenger tube from the guard, opened it, read the document, his eyes brightening, "This is glad tidings. My kingdom suffered greatly when all the mines played out. What else do you bring us?"

"The man responsible for three deaths, and three attempts to murder the landlords of the leystone mine," she let the bubble set the apothecary down gently, directing it to strip the leystone necklace when it did so, "He attempted to kill me as I carried the treaty to you, King. He admitted to killing the parents and brother of the current landlords. He entreated me to let him murder the last members of the

57

family," as an afterthought she added, directing her elemental to drop the necklace into the guard's hand, "He mined illegally on land which isn't his. This necklace is proof of his crime."

The king glared down at the man, "Their parents served as spies for my army, their brother as one of my loyal knights. Guards, take this scoundrel away for interrogation. There may be more foul deeds done by his hand."

Mary waited until only the king and the mayor remained.

"I must admit defeat to a quest given to me," she ignored the mayor's frantic look.

"What quest? Is there a beast you could not best?" The king looked worried.

"No. The mayor set me to catch a rabbit without magic nor the aid of my companion, Waterfall within one day's time. I managed to capture a rabbit, but gave it to the Stonesieges instead."

The king blinked at her, "A rabbit? Was this an evil rabbit?"

"No."

The king turned on the mayor, "You sent a champion, a magical champion after a rabbit?"

"Uncle, she..." The mayor started.

"Silence. I can see it in your eyes. You are fortunate Lady Mary recognizes a better quest for her skills. You will be coming back with me, nephew. You need to learn better leadership. Guard!"

One rushed back in a few minutes later, "My king?"

"Escort my nephew to his quarters so he may pack. He is coming with us. Go, nephew."

The mayor followed meekly behind the guard.

"Lady Mary. Please excuse his behavior. I release you from your quest debt to my kingdom. Ask me what I may give you as compensation for the insult."

She opened her mouth, then shut it.

The only thing she wanted, he couldn't give her. Only Gerard could.

"May I get some coin to ensure I have some for the next dwarven clan I come across?" She finally requested.

The king laughed, "All you want is some coins to pay you back for the food you bought the dwarves?"

"Yes."

He pulled out a pouch, handed it to her, "If you need any aid, contact me. This money is pale beside the insult you suffered."

"I am not doing these quests for the people yet. I am still Siren at heart. If Waterfall had not intervened, you would have a dead man instead of a live criminal. This is all I deserve right now."

"I think that is why King Gerard sent me with a missive for you."

"Missive?" Not another quest, she groused mentally.

"He told me to deliver this letter to you personally. I think he saw you needed someone here who would hear your side," he pulled out a sealed letter, "even heroes need fellow champions to help them."

She took the letter, broke the seal.

Another quest as she feared. King Silva of the lizard kingdom called her to deal with something besieging his kingdom.

"Where are you being summoned to?"

"To King Silva," she refolded the letter and tucked the letter in with the others Gerard sent her.

She would never admit when she felt alone, she read them to give her hope.

"Then let's travel together. I want to visit the Stonesieges and the children you defended. Then you can come spend a night at my castle where my men will prepare more supplies for you before you set out."

Straightening, Mary nodded, "I will welcome supplies and a nice bed."

They walked out together.

Part III
Siren's Shield

Mary arrived to the cavern city of King Silva at last.

When this quest came in she just finished a grueling set of adventures involving yet more quests.

To arrive, she traveled through a cursed forest, stopped a war, and defeated a clan of large trolls. She found herself exhausted before starting this quest.

Waterfall, her constant companion and mount whined, "There's hardly any water."

Mary dismounted the kelpie, wincing at the jolt her knee gave her.

The healer hadn't been too thrilled to treat Siren's dislocated knee. To tend the villainess who flooded several kingdoms in his tent. He never saw her as Lady Mary, champion of the hundred kingdoms seeking healing.

Ahead of her, a seven foot tall, dark grey lizard in dull silver metal armor slid through a door before it shut tight.

"What do you want?" he demanded of Mary.

"I am here at King Gerard's request to aid King Silva. I am Lady Mary," she bowed her head.

He considered her, then cocked his head.

"You're too short to be Lady Mary. Lady Mary is a great mage, in both stature and power."

She opened her mouth to tell off the guard when the door opened again.

A young pale green female lizard in a thin frock depicting the Priestesses of Flame whispered to the guard hurriedly.

He looked at Mary, his bright red neck frill flaring out, "This is Siren?"

Mary growled, "I am both. If you aren't going to let me by, at least get word to King Silva I have arrived."

Her tone made him straighten, put his hand on his sheathed sword.

The priestess hissed, her dark blue frill shaking, "Let her in. We have need of her. The flames say so."

Considering fire magic left pale scars over her hands, Mary doubted fire would say anything of the sort. However, she kept silent.

The guard growled, "She is a puny human. Nothing she does can help us."

Waterfall came forward, "Can we leave? This is no fun and they don't need us."

The guard and the priestess argued in low voices, their speech devolving into their native language.

Mary's patience ran out, so she reached for the nearest water source.

A fountain, by the feel of it, controlled the ebb and flow of water in a specific pattern.

Her elemental took joy in destroying that order, towering over the fountain.

Suddenly lizards ran by her, screaming in terror.

She blinked, looked pass them, through the open doors.

Her elemental towered in a thick mist. She didn't summon the mist.

Waterfall trumpeted, charged forward, scattering lizards from her path.

Mary heard a child's scream and ran forward, ordering her elemental to find the child and protect it.

A part of the mist turned red and blood scented the air as her elemental rushed down into a section still white.

The elemental pulled up, circling three children in a watery bubble.

Mary tried to disperse the mist, but it contained no water.

Then as quickly as it came, the mist vanished, leaving a crumpled lizard on the smooth floor.

Mary rushed to the lizard, muttering a healing spell she learned from a soldier on the front lines. It may give her time to get a healer.

She sank beside the lizard and realized the spell wouldn't help this female. Her black eyes already filmed over with death.

Mary looked up at her elemental, "Bring the children down, gently."

The bubble floated down, then set the children on the ground.

Once the bubble popped, they rushed to the lizard, keening.

"This is their mother," the priestess stated as she knelt, closing dead eyes, "Go in peace, my sister. Your line continues and you will be avenged."

"Lady Mary?" King Silva's voice drew up her eyes.

She stared as he strode toward her, ten guards with him. He towered above them by a good foot in height, his dull red skin matched with a vivid purple frill covered in gold ornaments of his kingship. His bright green robe flowed around him as he paused above the dead female.

"King Gerard sent me here. I didn't know there was an attack in progress until your people ran by me."

Waterfall clopped back to them, "The mist vanished into ground. I could not follow."

She looked down at the body, the three crying children, lowered her head in shame and sorrow.

Mary stood, looking up into Silva's black eyes, "We need to speak, King Silva."

He nodded, "Gerard would not send you unless your strength is needed. Priestess, would you escort the young lady's body to my healer?"

The priestess nodded, "I will, my king."

Silva turned to the guard who'd blocked Mary, "Please take the children back to their nest. Ensure their relatives are made aware of this."

"Yes, my king," the guard gently pried the children from the body, carrying the smallest as he led them away, the other two clutching his tail.

Mary walked with Silva, Waterfall at her back as they left the scene, noting his people hid in their caves, shutting doors as their party approached.

Fear flowed through the streets in place of people.

She turned to Silva, "This has been going on a while, hasn't it, King Silva?"

His frilled flared angrily for a moment, then relaxed, "I would like to hear what you observed, Lady Mary."

A little shame went through her at her actions to force the guard to let her in. A childish impulse to instill fear into him for his disrespect rather than goodness.

"I arrived and spoke to the guard you sent the children with. He didn't believe me Lady Mary or Siren as I am so short. Your Priestess of Flame came and argued with him I'm myself. This went on for some time."

Silva smiled, "Then you summoned your water elemental so you could slip inside while my guards fought the elemental?"

She hung her head, "It wasn't befitting a champion."

He laughed, "I did something similar during my adventuring days. Please continue."

She raised an eyebrow at him, "I thought your people fled my elemental, though it was too soon for that. When I looked, mist covered the entire area. Waterfall charged forward before I realized children stood in danger. I ordered my elemental to secure them. The mist turned red where the body lay. Before I could enter the mist, it cleared rapidly. The elemental held the children in the air, protected while I focused on the downed female. By the time I got to her side, she was dead."

He frowned, "What did you think of the mist?"

"It's not water."

He stopped making her pause, "It wasn't water?"

"No, I tried dispersing it so I could see the attacker. It contained no water in it. I would have fed the mist into my elemental if it had been."

"Interesting, we thought the mist spelled by whatever is causing these attacks."

Mary focused on that, "How many attacks so far?"

"Five including today's."

"I need to hear about these other attacks. Perhaps I can help with my knowledge," Gerard might have sent her as she'd been a villainess.

While trapped in her tower, she read from the massive library her predecessors collected. It'd been very eclectic.

Silva continued walking, "The first happened about a month ago. A woman of my people belonging to the sorcerer line. She could summon acidic bubbles. Guards found her body in the morning, surrounded by acid burns on the floor and walls. Whatever attacked her, didn't fear acid."

She calculated a death a week, or close to it.

"No one witnessed the attack?"

He shook his head, "None. The second attack came a few days later, a young child, also adult. Her mother and grandmother grew worried and went looking. They entered a mist which made them nervous. The mist cleared to reveal their child, barely alive. She didn't last until morning."

Waterfall rubbed her head on Mary's shoulder, "I don't want to be here."

Mary petted Waterfall's head, "The third attack came shortly on the heels of the second?"

"No, it came a week later, in the middle of our Festival of Freedom. No one noticed at first, but mist slowly filled the lanes of our market," he led Mary into a wide area with stalls, "I stood on the stage there," he indicated a raised platform made of layered rock slabs, "When I noticed the mist, it was too late. The mist turned red in the middle of the plaza. My guards rushed the area, but we couldn't see who attacked or the victim under assault. As quickly as the attack began, the mist cleared. An elderly woman lay dead. We were so focused on her and calming the panicked crowd we didn't notice the screams coming from down the street."

Mary could see how it infuriated Silva as his frills stayed flared, trembling with his rage.

"Another female?"

"No, a man. He defended his nest, which held six baby girls. We arrived as he fought off the attacker with a torch. We could see it flashing over the mist as he swung it. He cried out as we rushed forward, then the mist vanished. He lay bleeding, gasping for breath. I remember his babies crowding him, wailing as he died."

Something hunted his people and he powerless to stop it.

She looked at him, "No attacks until today?"

He nodded, "I hoped it killed by the last victim. It seems that is not so."

"I'll help you hunt this thing down," she promised, "as much information as we can share, the better we can identify the killer and bring him, her or it to justice."

He looked at her, "You sound like Gerard from our days as champions."

She frowned, as Waterfall snickered.

"Come with me, milady," Silva led the way towards what had to be his palace. Rock walls reached the cavernous roof, every inch of them carved with regal figures of lizards fighting trolls, dragons and others lizards.

They passed under a grand archway to find the same stillness as on the streets. No one moved about, hiding in their elaborate caves, behind beaded or leather curtains.

"Have any other champions come to deal with this?"

"No, we locked ourselves in. Stopped all caravans coming in or going out. Word would spread quickly if we let them out. The merchants here are local and too afraid to leave, aiding us in the silence. There are rumors this mist is from outside the city and came following someone. Others say we grew too prideful of being the true rulers of the reptile kingdom, instead of dragons."

"Why would that cause this?"

"Dragons claim they are the rulers, but they do not descended directly from Sishlash, the first ruler of all reptiles. We are. The rumors say because we killed the black dragon who ruled your kingdom, we showed too much pride and Sishlash sent the mist to remind us we should be humble."

"That is ridiculous. The dragon grew too prideful and given his downfall by his own actions. Whatever is doing this, is here to sow discord and to kill."

"I agree," Silva turned them into a tunnel leading sharply downward.

The air grew colder.

They entered a room with rock tables stretching into darkness.

"This is where we prepare the dead. You will see the body of the latest to fall."

"Are the bodies of the other victims here?" She tried to recall the lizard's burial rituals.

"Only the man," he looked at her, "The bodies of our other victims vanished since the examinations."

"Vanished?" She looked at Silva, realized he spoke of it where other ears could not hear.

"The attendant of the dead came to prepare them after cleansing, but the bodies were gone."

"May I see the body you do have?"

He led her to a covered table in the dark, a couple of his guards taking up torches to light the way.

Silva pulled back the cover.

Lacerations covered the male lizard, arcing as if carved by claws. His grey skin cut deeply, even to the bone in many places by whoever or whatever attacked him.

"He died a warrior," Silva made a gesture of respect, "We all wish to die defending our home and family with honor."

"This attacker clawed him," she looked at the deepest wound, "Did you recover any claws from the wounds?"

"None. We looked for such things first. Unlike the other bodies, his showed more violence and brutality in his wounds. They did not like him."

Mary straightened, "Why do you say that?"

"The women fought, but didn't die harshly. As if once the attacker got through their defenses, they treated the women...tenderly is wrong but fits. The man they tore into, as if he denied them something."

"Silva, I think you're right. Let's suppose the target was his babies and your fallen warrior got in their way. They, whoever they are, were stopped by him. They go after your women, and this one fought them off. It would make them angry. Instead of doing what they did with women, they attacked physically," she looked at the claw marks, noting most wounds grouped in fours, "May I examine his entire body?"

Silva nodded, backing up.

She pulled down the cover to look over his arms.

His right lay shredded, as if he'd blocked many attacks with his forearm. She noticed something strange on the wrist of the other arm.

It bore the four clawed grooves on one side, but a single claw mark on the other side.

She held her hand over the wound, noticed the claw marks lined up with her fingers, though from a much wider hand.

"Found something?" Silva asked, startling Mary.

She took a breath to calm her racing heart, "Yes. Notice my hand and these five claw marks?"

He looked, blinked then laid his own hand over hers. His hand splayed wider than the marks.

"Something gripped his wrist, and he must have pulled away," he summarized.

She realized she gone an extra step he hadn't.

One of his people killed this one. However, she knew their claws broke off with deep wounds, especially if they struck bone.

Perhaps like his frill ornaments, someone covered their claws with metal, to prevent breakage.

"Were the victims related to each other?"

"This one and first victim married ages ago. The others have less of a connection."

She turned as the guards came to attention.

The Priestess escorted the body of the latest victim with gravity and dignity.

Another lizard joined her, wearing black robes signifying him as an attendant of the dead.

Mary walked over, watching them clean the body.

No wounds she could see. The body had a pale look to it.

"She is like the others. Bloodless," Silva commented.

Mary turned to Silva, "Bloodless?"

"The women, to the last, drained of all blood, but no wounds could be accounted for the loss."

She looked down as they finished cleaning the body, "Do you have a map where the attacks took place?"

"I'll send for the map," Silva nodded to one of his guards, who took off running, "What else?"

"I would like to cast a spell to see if magic drained her blood."

"There are spells able to do that?"

She looked at him, puzzled, "Yes. That's how I knew a spell caster would come calling. They killed a monster in my forest it would be teleported to my tower. Then I knew if I faced a physical based champion or not."

"Where did you get the spell?"

"Spell Discovery Volume Five," she saw his face change, "Is something wrong?"

"That book was lost to us over a hundred years ago. A dark lord purchased all of volume five and destroyed them."

She thought about it, then shrugged, "I don't see why. There were many spells like the one to detect magic."

"That is the point. If magic can be detected in say a goblet, then a ruler won't succumb to the spell and die."

Mary opened her mouth to argue when she heard a cry behind her.

Whirling, she froze at the grisly image of the attendant to the dead being gnawed on by the dead body.

Mary acted before the undead attacked the Priestess of Flame.

Her elemental seized the priestess and shot out of the room as the guards drew their swords and advanced on the undead.

"What is it?"

"Undead. Some sort of bloodsucker," Mary tackled Silva, throwing them both sideways and under a bench.

Rock shattered as the undead plowed through the tables, tearing up guards on the way.

"Freeze it," Silva ordered as Mary gathered her power.

Waterfall trumpeted, slammed into the undead, sending it across the floor.

She tried to trample it, but it moved fast, scurrying along the floor, then up the wall.

Its claws glinted like iron as the undead clung to the ceiling with fingers and toes, its malevolent eyes flashing red in the torchlight.

"Asanbosam," Mary breathed.

"What?" Silva hissed.

"Fire. Its weakness is fire."

Mary struggled to remember a fire spell which wouldn't lash back at her brutally, yet still deal with the bloodsucker.

The thing launched itself over Waterfall's head at Mary. She formed an ice wall between her and it, knowing it would plow through.

Orange, red and brilliant white flared beyond her wall, followed by a horrible scream.

"Waterfall!" Mary cried in alarm.

"I'm alright. The thing is ashes now," Waterfall snorted, "I couldn't hurt it."

Mary dropped the ice barrier, returning it to liquid form.

Dirty piles of what looked like mud, splattered the floor.

"Who burned it?" Mary asked.

Silva stood up, offered his hand, "I did. I am a strong practitioner of fire magic. It is why I was chosen to rule."

She took his hand, stood, "I don't know how much use I'll be against the Asanbosom. It doesn't fear water nor is it harmed by water spells."

"What is an Asanbosom?"

"A vampire-like being. It's usually human, though it looks like it can be lizard as well. Its nails become iron and clawed. The toes also gain the same iron claw look. They normally attack their prey from trees and haul them up into the branches. Here, it allows them to scale walls. This type belongs to a kingdom in a forested area. They wouldn't travel here as there is no trees to hang from."

"Then we work together. Your knowledge, my magic."

One of the surviving guards protested, "My king. We have three fire magi who could assist Lady Mary on this hunt. We cannot risk you."

"Everyone is at risk from this. I will not cower in my nest like a newborn while my people suffer. Come, Lady Mary. We will see what you think of the map."

Waterfall hung her head, "I will be of no use."

"You can get me to where I need to faster than I can walk. That will save my strength for what lays ahead."

Including the protection of King Silva, who acted too eager for combat. She almost thought he wanted to go out fighting like he did with King Gerard before they took control of their kingdoms. It meant he'd take risks a younger lizard could get out of, but an older lizard may die from.

Following King Silva to his war room, she examined the map he unrolled.

The dots made no pattern she could see. A dot sat near the entrance to the city, another at what looked to be a university based on the symbol beside it, one in the plaza, one near the smiths section of town, and the final one near the palace walls.

"This thing attacks widely," she noted, leaning over the map, "Rich, poor, influential, educated. It doesn't have a preference."

"Except women," Silva snarled, his frill trembling as he glared at each dot.

"I propose we set out bait," Mary decided on a plan to lure the infernal thing out.

"Who would you send to slaughter?" he snapped.

"Me."

***

A seamstress worked quickly on Mary's new clothes. Her orange scales flushed a darker color when Mary looked over to gauge the progress.

Mary fiddled with the leystone she carried, wondering if she could force the mist to disperse with a well placed shield of air.

If Silva could see the enemy from a distance, he could burn them with his magic.

His guards loved this plan, however Silva did not.

"Your robe is ready, my lady," the seamstress lisped as she held out the clothing.

Mary touched it, nodded, "This will do well. Let's see if the attacker likes humans."

Donning the robe over her traveling leathers, Mary looked in the mirror.

She looked like a wealthy lady except her eyes. Her eyes said, "I'm not prey. Attack me if you dare."

"May I add some adornments?" The seamstress turned red when Mary looked at her.

"The earrings on one ear, the rings and the necklaces are not enough?"

"You are playing a lady here to marry with our king, no? You need to look like as a princess."

Mary nodded, "What do you suggest?"

Silva stalked in ten minutes later, "When will you be ready?"

Then his frills flared as he caught sight of her as the seamstress wove a gold braid through her brown hair.

"I look that unusual?" Mary asked, an eyebrow up, the chains from the circlet chiming as they shifted across her brow.

"You look regal," he leaned down, "This will work."

"You can thank your seamstress. She recommended this look."

"She walks well," the seamstress said with a hum, "She wouldn't fear the mist as new arrival."

"She didn't bring a guard," Silva pointed out.

"Princess Hala and Lady Clashsah go without guards even now," the seamstress chirped back.

"Just go along with it, King Silva. You know this is our best chance to capture the beast."

"Very well. I'll go prepare my court."

He left.

"He finds you very catching," the seamstress whispered.

"Only due to your recommendations."

"He finds you dangerous. You remind him of his days as champion."

Mary rolled her eyes, "Why is he hung up on that?"

"He left so he could learn to be good king. He traveled alone for a time before King Gerard met him on a quest to kill a maiden-eating dragon. They became blood brothers. Defeated enemies greater than themselves alone, until Silva received the call from home."

Mist flooded the room.

Mary grabbed the seamstress, pulled her behind her back.

"Pretty young lady," a voice whispered out of the mist.

"You should address me as proper to a woman of my rank," Mary hoped she could delay the Asanbosom until Silva returned.

"I've heard in the streets you are Lady Mary. Further words say you are a princess here to marry the King," the voice crooned.

So Silva's spies managed to spread the story they concocted to tempt the undead to attack.

"Then you should address me as royal highness," Mary scanned the mist, hoping to see the speaker.

"Your royal highness, it is a pleasure to met a human after so long."

"What do you mean?"

"Please call me Lord Salorn," he whispered.

She preferred Gerard's seduction. Straight-forward and confident.

"Very well, Lord Salorn. What do you mean?"

"These lands are populated with only lizards. Only female blood soothes the thirst. Their bodies are hard and unfriendly."

The seamstress trembled, clutching Mary's robe.

"Then why not leave? Why not go where you want, Lord Salorn."

"Ah, your royal highness," he chuckled, "I think you clever. I can feel him coming."

She threw up the air shield, thrusting the mist away.

Four female lizards, no Asanbosoms, clung to the ceiling of the room, eyes hungrily on Mary and the seamstress.

"An air whisperer," mist clung to the far corner, resisting her air shield.

"You will not find me easy prey, Lord Salorn," she haughtily stated, "I will not go willingly like these women."

The seamstress screamed.

Mary whirled, saw two of the Asanbosoms pulling her upward by her frill. Mary shot out icicles into their wrists, forcing them to drop the seamstress.

"You dare to attack my seamstress?" Mary felt the leystone draining as she fought to keep the air shield up against the mist.

"I can see why he covets you," the thicker mist trembled, "We shall see if you like me when he is defeated."

Then they vanished into the mist, leaving only splotches of blood on the floor.

Silva slammed open the door, sweeping the room with his eyes.

Mary sat down, her legs trembling from the magic she pushed out for an element she didn't command.

The seamstress blubbered in panic, clutching her torn robe to her shoulders.

"They were here?" Silva hissed.

"Yes. We have a name. Lord Salorn. He prefers the female blood of your people because it is the only one to sooth his bloodlust."

Silva went to the seamstress, got her standing then passed her over to his guards.

"He didn't attack you?"

"You spread my title well. He knew it, but not I am a champion."

"There are sixteen Lady Mary's and you are known for your water skills. He must have assumed you are another Mary since you fought him with air."

"I used ice to free the seamstress from the females he's changed."

"You are the only one I know who can't call on the other elements without a leystone, even for a few moments. He won't assume you are Siren."

"He seems to view you as competition."

Silva grinned, "I'm quite popular with the ladies."

She glared at him, "You are enjoying this too much."

"You got the leader here in less than a day. If we work it, we can catch him."

"He is able to cloak himself with the mist. I couldn't see him. He could be a lizard, but he seemed to miss humans."

"Is it possible he was human?"

"Then why is he here, tormenting your people? I can't figure it out."

"We'll find out. Until then, you aren't leaving my side."

Mary scowled at him, "You think it will help?"

He slid a hand around her waist, "You are desired by him and I have you. He'll come."

***

Mary began to hate Silva.

He intentionally left his guards behind throughout the next three days. She stopped him from drinking poison, pricking his fingers on bespelled jewelry, or taking daggers to the back.

She collapsed into her bed, glad the seamstress' robes were light and didn't restrict movement.

A knock sounded.

She muffled a groan, got up.

Opening the door, she found Silva there, without his guards again.

"Are you trying to get killed?" She asked glaring at him.

"I bring a note from Gerard for you."

She took the letter, broke the seal as she rushed over to the light.

As she read the words, she realized Gerard sent her encouragement this time.

"I know by the time you read this, you'll be quite tired of Silva's lust for the glory days. He misses the days we adventured together and didn't have to fight with words, but with swords and magic. You are the pillar standing between him and a premature death. Your strengths will balance his weakness. You'll be one large step closer to your freedom with this quest. Remember your water is not weak against your foe. You just need to outsmart the defenses of your opponent. I look forward to seeing you happy and with child. Remember two, hopefully a boy and a girl."

She smiled, rereading the letter.

"Why did Gerard save you?"

She looked over at Silva, his keen eyes focused on her.

She folded the letter, decided to tell him a partial truth, "He saw past the scars and villainy defining me as Siren to the mother I'll become and the wife to be."

Silva chuckled, "He loves children, and happy endings."

"He may not see mine if Lord Salorn continues to run amok."

"Sleep. We'll have better luck tomorrow."

"Like the prior days."

He brushed her hair back with a claw, "It looks darkest before dawn breaks."

Then he surprised her by kissing her forehead, then closing the door at his back.

Tired, she turned back to her bed.

Only to be surrounded by mist.

Then she felt her breath stolen from her lungs.

***

She woke slowly, fuzzy as to what happened to her.

"I didn't want him interrupting us like last time, my royal highness."

She jerked up, turned to the voice.

Mist surrounded Mary, making anything beyond the bed she sat on indistinct.

"I don't accept invitations via kidnapping, Lord Salorn."

"I think you would accept this," iron scrapped her nape, making her whirl around.

An iron gauntlet vanished into the mist, pitted on the thumb as if scored by acid.

An acid bubble must have glanced his hand.

"You are more than Silva can appreciate. You guard his back with coy glances and spells."

His gauntlet seized her ankle, making her jerk before she realized she couldn't move him. His physical strength surpassed hers.

"You're right," she figured to play his game, gain time to think of a better way out of this, "He doesn't see danger from a goblet, a scarf given as a gift, a knife his friend carries. I suppose nothing hurts you."

He released her ankle, the claws playfully scrapping her skin, "He doesn't see you. You would never need to guard my back. I rather guard yours as you grow stronger," his claws splayed, dug into the bed around her ankle, "Each year you live, more iron covers your fragile skin. Until every bit is covered in armor."

Swallowing, she shook her head, "I don't need iron armor. I can have steel, gold, silver made to fit me."

"I see, my royal highness. It's a pity I do not have more time to speak with you this night."

Mary worried he'd turn her then and there, "Why is that, Lord Salorn?"

"I must weaken Silva so the populace turns against him. He lost his bride, and now he'll lose his most trusted advisor. Until tomorrow, my royal highness," the mist swirled, then dispersed.

She looked over the walls of her prison and realized she faced solid rock, with tiny openings only a mouse could fit through.

Angry she'd been captured and on the path to becoming an Asanbosom herself, she cursed Gerard for not being clear on what to expect.

Standing, she explored her cell, touching each nook and cranny in hope of a secret door.

Hours later, if her cell hid a secret door, it kept its location from her.

Sitting back on the bed, her stomach grumbled and she felt thirsty.

She coaxed her elemental to gather a few sips of water for her to drink. As Mary contemplated her dire situation, slowly sipping the water gathered for her, she wondered what she could do to lead Silva to the Asanbosom. With fire, he could roast them all in an eye blink.

If only the mist from the Asanbosom could be followed.

She sat upright.

Summoning her water elemental she told it to lay a path of mist out of the cell and to find Silva.

The people would be terrified of seeing a line of mist, but hopefully Silva would recall she said the mist the undead cloaked themselves with did not come from water.

She sent the elemental out, praying it found Silva quickly.

***

She woke from a doze to see mist oozing inside her cell.

"I thought we were past this, Lord Salorn."

"I am not my lord," a female hissed, "You are not one of his."

"No, however he does intend to make me his," Mary countered.

Mary barely dodged the flash of claws as it passed through where she sat.

Standing besides the bed, Mary tried to keep her attacker in front of her.

This turned out to be impossible as the mist muffled sound and veiled sight.

Mary yelped as claws raked her back, making her leap unto the bed, trying to defend herself.

"Stop!"

The mist pulled back and Mary got her first good look at Lord Salorn.

He must have started life as a large human. He certainly did not look like the lizards. Iron covered every part of him, starting with his scythe-like toes and ending at the crown of his head. When he spoke she could see the only part of him not sheathed with iron. His mouth.

"You dare to attack my royal highness?"

Mary began to hate him for thinking she belonged to him. She didn't.

She belonged with Gerard.

The female cowered in the corner, "Please, milord. Let us please you, serve you. We are worthy."

"Enough. You would damage my prize. You would kill the only human I've met since coming to this wasteland. You are not to harm her again. None of you."

Mary turned then sat on the bed's headboard.

Three more females stood in the room, staring at her with jealousy.

What in the Hundred Kingdoms kept Silva from finding her?

He longed for his glory days, yet here she sat, a damsel in distress.

Well, she'd fight her way out if needed. Rock parted for water. Both she and her elemental still possessed strength to blow out a section of a mountain to escape.

Her elemental returned, oozing through a crack.

Right then the floor dropped, sending her, the bed and the female Asanbosoms plummeting.

Her water elemental surrounded her in a bubble, knocking aside rubble and the claws of the females as they tried to strike her.

Then flame shot pass her water to steam half her shield away.

With a splash, her bubble broke, drenching her in cool relief.

She sat in the fountain near the city gates.

Looking up she saw Silva and several others sprinting towards her, their flames lashing overhead, vaporizing falling debris.

Her cell had been in the roof of the cavern, right over the fountain.

"Where is Lord Salorn?" Silva demanded once he stood beside the fountain.

"Yes, I'm alright, King Silva," she snapped, "No, the undead lord didn't outright kill me."

"I'll hear that later," he ordered.

"You'll hear it now, you damn big snake!" Mary stood, angry with him, "I've been knocking aside all the attempts on your life since you ordered your guards away and you don't even have the decency to be waiting for the damn Asanbosom to show up in your palace! You make me wait for a damn rescue while his harem tried to kill me and he played seducer. It's a wonder you lived to be king."

Silva gaped, so astonished he dropped his flame elemental. The others stared in disbelief.

She turned and pointed up at the hovering mist, "And you are a disgrace. You want to win me, well you should impress me. Kidnapping me like a scoundrel, letting your harem attack me then turning around and trying to soothe my ruffled feathers like a child is demeaning. You aren't worth half the one I love."

She went and said what tangled her heart in knots for a couple months now.

Mary loved Gerard even with his cryptic messages in the midst of letters to her. Only her.

The mist descended, then parted to show Lord Salorn, his hands curled into claws.

His eyes locked on Silva, "Even with your untimely rescue, I look the fool. It's time to end this."

Flames burst from the ground engulfing the Asanbosom. Mary liked seeing those flames consuming the one who frightened her and made her weak. She may forgive Silva, in time.

Then hair raising laughter echoed in the cavern.

Through the flames Lord Salorn strode, as if the flames posed no threat.

"I grew out of my weakness to flame long ago, Silva. I'll impress Princess Mary by killing you and showing love to a weak man is nothing compared to a god."

"Siren, combine with me as you did Gerard against the dragon."

She didn't question Silva so she summoned her water elemental around her, making it grow into a tower.

"You think to drown me?" Then Lord Salorn backed up, "Siren?"

She thrust her water elemental into his mouth, Silva's fire boiling through into the Asanbosom.

Steam roared as it poured from Lord Salorn, carrying a foul stench with it.

A time later a clang sounded.

Mary pulled back her elemental, felt Silva do the same.

All which remained of Lord Salorn lay in iron pieces: his skin.

Mary sat in the fountain, letting her elemental go sucking water from around her.

She'd survived. This damsel managed to kill another tormentor. With a little help.

"Now what were you saying about me leaving you to face him alone," Silva hissed, towered over her, his frill flared like a cobra about to strike.

She fumed, "Exactly what I said. You hound your glory days without thinking you are King now. You can't go galavanting after every dark mage, foul beast or daring adventure. You are the pillar of your people. You die, civil war erupts."

Silva considered her for a long moment, then sighed, his frill folding back.

"I miss those days. Simpler times. Your enemies came at you from the front, with few from the side or behind. I didn't need advisors, guards nor champions to do what needed to be dealt with."

He sat on the edge of the fountain, "I miss being on the road with my blood brother, traveling where he saw we needed to be."

Mary laid a hand on his shoulder, "You are needed here as king, not as champion. Leave the champion business to someone like me."

He looked at her, "You should be married with a horde of babies running around."

"You offering?"

"No. My ladies would skin me alive if I really married you," he stood, took her hand and pulled her to her feet, "Let's get you a warm meal and a healer."

"I prefer a bathroom," she admitted, "They were quite uncivilized."

He laughed, "Ah, but one day this tale shall inspire your children to go out on their own adventures."

"Or scare them into staying home," she rubbed her neck.

Feeling only one necklace made her pause.

"You are free of six debts by my count," Silva tsked at her, "You better clear the rest before you are an old maid."

He laughed and didn't see the ice she laid under his feet. He slipped and fell on his face.

"Don't you know anything, Silva. Old maids are the most dangerous women around."

Waterfall clopped up, her mouth clamped on a sealed letter.

Another quest.

Mary would kill Gerard once she saw him again.

Part IV

Siren's Fury

Mary dismounted Waterfall, glad to be back inside the Hundred Kingdoms.

The beast she'd chased through the Frigid Desert merrily led her around until she got a hunting party formed.

It took her six months to do it. She needed a giant, three trolls, a hedge witch and a elf to do it, but she'd done it. Who knew trolls hated Syd Hounds and would even agree to a cease fire to hunt them down?

She walked with Waterfall into the capital city of Gharldha, who's king sent her letters every few weeks, even out in the Frigid Desert.

A red plumed guard strode over to her, "I'm sorry but you have to hold the reins of your mount while in the city, miss."

She stared at him for a long moment, looked at Waterfall, then back at him.

"You want me to hold the reins of a kelpie through the entire city? For what reason?"

The guard's eyes went round, looked at Waterfall who leaned down to nuzzle the hand of a brave boy, then Mary's single last earring on her right ear, the remaining necklace and the two dozen rings covering her hands.

He bowed, "I apologize, Lady Mary. I meant no offense."

Waterfall nudged Mary when she didn't immediately respond.

"At ease. I suggest you pay more mind to who you approach. The next one may not be so forgiving."

When had she become so good she no longer thought of instilling fear into people she crossed?

It didn't matter. She wanted to go find Gerard and strangle him for sending her such a troublesome quest.

Dropping a coin into the boy's hand, ruffling his hair before she joined the throng, she continued to the palace.

"You could have dumped him in the fountain," Waterfall mused.

"Ruining that water for children? No."

The next guard she encountered knew her.

"Lady Mary. Did you hear about the new kingdom?"

Another quest? She mentally sighed as she shook her head, "Whispers once I got out of the Frigid Desert. What is the tale making the rounds?"

"Joined about five months ago under King Amerith, then at the party to join the Hundred Kingdoms, his brother stabbed him in the back. Said brother killed himself next to start a civil war. Unfortunately for him, his niece ascended to the throne. She's only fourteen and a handful, so I've heard."

"So we are the Hundred and One Kingdoms now?" At least Mary didn't owe this new kingdom a debt for killing their champions.

"For now. My relief just arrived so I can escort you to the king."

"Good."

She could strangle him finally.

Waterfall frolicked away to a pond the guard said she could play in.

A few minutes later Mary stood in a short line to enter King Gerard's office, with one person in front of her.

He was called into the office leaving her to wait impatiently.

When Gerard wanted something, he got it right this instant. She spent months to get a single piece of jewelry off.

Looking at her hands and the alternating bands of metal and her skin, she hoped she could be free of the debts each represented. So, she could hold the baby one day she'd have.

"Lady Mary, the king is ready to see you," the herald held open the door.

She strode in, noting with satisfaction the herald exited and closed the door so she and Gerard were alone.

He looked drawn, as if he'd not slept for weeks.

She forgot her anger as she sat down opposite him, "Why haven't you been sleeping?"

He sat back, rubbed his shoulders, "My visions are a blessing and a burden. I've been receiving constant portents of destruction and death from our newest kingdom. They are growing stronger."

She saw it in his eyes. He needed to send her but didn't want to.

"I have to go?"

He stood walked to a glassed over arrow slit, "Once I see a happy ending, it's usually so strong it can't be undone."

Her heart lurched. He intended her to march to her death to protect all the kingdoms.

"I see two paths for this danger in Barnarthi. If you are not sent, lava will rush from the kingdom, burning everything in fifty of the kingdoms, killing people in all but two remaining kingdoms. You'll lead the survivors and raise two beautiful children, but I will die in the first three months."

She frowned at his back, wishing he'd tell this to her face.

"If you are sent, whatever is brewing will abate, however a new evil will attempt to take control of Barnarthi, and I will die facing it. You will live and have a daughter who will rule for fifty years after your reign."

She slowly got to her feet, "You said."

"My happy visions usually stay as they appear, letting me know if tiny touches are needed to adjust back to full happiness. I've thought of every possible action I could take to stop my death, but I can't. All that matters is the Hundred and One Kingdoms survive and you live to your happy ending."

Mary gritted her teeth, fear swamping her.

She didn't fight trolls, mages and other villains just to lose the one she loved.

"There is always another way," she stated harshly, "This champion duty forced on me has shown me that. Together we bested a black dragon. We can best this."

He shook his head, "I already thought of that. If I go with you, I will still die, but all the kingdoms will perish in lava."

"Good men do not give up," she strode around his desk, seized his forearm, "I didn't fight through all those damn quests to lose you now."

He looked at her, "My time is set. The vision of us together is gone."

"Perhaps another seer can..." He pulled her into him and kissed her.

It felt like a goodbye as he released her.

"Go and save the dreams of all little girls."

She straightened, her heart breaking as she realized he said the one thing that would make her go.

Releasing his arm, she turned around and strode to the door.

Before she opened it, she snapped, "Good wins, Gerard. You taught me that."

Storming down the halls she drew her anger over the hurt. He gave up on them being together, having a child. All because of some lava.

Waterfall ran over the instant Mary cleared the door, "Something wrong?"

Mary turned to one of the guards, "Which way to Barnarthi?"

He gulped at her murderous expression, "Take the west road all the way to Bales Road. Then head south until you get to the mountains. Beyond those mountains is Barnarthi."

She waited for Waterfall to be saddled, supplied, then she swung into the saddle.

Looking up, she saw only a flicker of light on the arrow slit to Gerard's study.

If she turned the lava aside, she'd lose him, forever.

She rode out, trying to outrun the betrayal of her dream.

***

Two weeks later, she crested the mountains to her first view of Barnarthi. She'd been there sooner if the small side quests hadn't slowed her.

According to rumors she heard, the new queen, Carlith, had a temper and her kingdom suffered from unusual heat. The traveling merchants said to bring lots of water as the locals would fleece you twice for a sip.

The land below her looked ready to catch fire and burn with no help from lava or a lightning strike.

"Too dry," Waterfall whined, "I don't feel so good around my mouth."

"It's a dry heat," Mary called her elemental to keep Waterfall wet, "Doesn't feel natural. Perhaps whoever is doing this is trying to control a fire elemental."

Waterfall started down the path, "You've been very dark since Gharldha. Is something wrong?"

"Enough is wrong I want to ensure it doesn't hurt the people I love."

It took them four hours to traverse the roads to the first city, which wasn't the capital as she expected. Her mood soured further when she found she needed to turn around to get to the capital.

She retraced her path to a crossroads, then took the left path for a full day to get to her destination.

A single mountain rose from the capital, emitting black smoke from its top.

Sensing a powerful spell under foot, she paused Waterfall to examine it. It drew on all the water underground to flood the mountain. Tracing it, she realized someone wanted to drown the spirit of fire living in the mountain.

Fire Spirits didn't take kindly to being drenched so Mary guessed this spirit would cause the destruction Gerard foretold. Mary broke the spell, righting the path of the water. Problem solved.

Waterfall and her arrived at the city to excited buzz.

"The fountains are working," a man bellowed as he ran by her, "Go get water before they run out again."

Mary promised to find the person behind the water spell and teach him, her or them to never attack a fire spirit again. Considering her mood, she'd enjoy it.

They walked to the palace and found no guards at the gate. Normally, one or more would challenge Mary. She missed it now as she could have taken her frustrations out on one of them.

The courtyard seemed less empty than the gate as a stable boy rushed out to take Waterfall's reins.

"No funny business this time, Waterfall," Mary cautioned, knowing if she didn't, the kelpie would take the boy to the nearest river or stream for a run.

Waterfall would see it as fun, the boy after he got off the ride alive would want to do it again, and the kingdom's inhabitants would eye Mary warily.

Stepping up the stairs to where she finally met guards, she wondered how to approach Queen Carlith.

"Who are you?"

Mary straightened, "I am Lady Mary, Champion of the Hundred and One Kingdoms. I've come to offer my services to the newest kingdom."

The guards looked at each other then to a boy leaning against the wall.

Not a boy, Mary corrected as he walked over.

The short man wore the same outfit as the guards, but exuded authority. His black eyes assessed her.

"I'm Sarith, head of the guard. We welcome Champion Mary. I'll escort you inside."

He seemed to smile at her with mischievousness. She made sure to watch everything.

She nodded to him, "I welcome the opportunity to meet Queen Carlith at her convenience."

They walked down a long, stuffy hallway.

They should summon an air elemental to sweep through. It would do wonders to improve the atmosphere.

Mary stepped into the audience room in time to see a fireball flying at a prostrating man.

Her water elemental rushed into a wall to defend the man. The fire extinguished the instant it touched her wall.

Mary stormed forward, looking for an attacker to deal harshly with.

Through the wall, she could see Carlith on her throne, flanked by two guards.

Mary summoned back her elemental, eyes scanning for threats.

"You may leave, horse master," Carlith sneered at the man, her flame-red hair braided back, "You owe a life debt to this woman."

The man stood, bowed repeatedly as he retreated.

Carlith stood on the dais, her diminutive height barely even with Mary as her black eyes locked with Mary's, "There are not many who command water elementals. There are fewer who can command such a powerful one. You must be Lady Mary, the one everyone fears and respects."

"I see my reputation proceeded me, Queen Carlith. I travelled far to offer my services to you and your people."

"I have no beast or villain for you to hunt down."

"Would you like me to find the one who poured the city's water into the mountain?" Mary could see Carlith would dismiss her shortly.

Carlith paused, "You broke the spell sending the water to the volcano?"

"I did. The water's path was impeded by magic. Someone like that could do great harm to your people if left unchecked."

The queen sat, beckoned Mary closer, "I would hear more of this."

Mary bowed, then approached the dais, "If it will not take away from your other duties, your Highness."

"I choose my duties," the tone cut the air with its bitterness.

"I meant no offense, your Highness," Mary spoke calmly, "I will convey what I know as briefly as I can. The spell caster sent the water into the mountain to drown the fire spirit living there, possibly to weaken it for a binding spell."

Carlith sneered, "They would fail even if they drained all the oceans in this world."

So the queen knew of the spirit.

"They diverted the water under your city to it and as I approached your walls, I sensed the spell. Since it seemed wrong, I severed the connection from the caster and righted the water to the path it preferred. The fountains recovered their splash to your people's delight. The people chatted excitedly while I walked your streets."

Carlith smiled, "You think the fire is caused by the villain who stole our water?"

Mary raised an eyebrow, "With so little evidence, I can only assume the caster of the fire was in this room and wanted the horse master dead."

"My queen," a harried fat man scurried in, "Please. The council needs your counsel."

"I will come when I am ready," she snapped at him, before she summoned a fireball and threw it at him.

Mary shielded him in time, understanding now why no one patrolled the streets. The guards worked on preventing the Queen from frying her own people.

"I would like to listen in, Queen Carlith. Perhaps the villain is causing other issues and I can find them faster."

Carlith frowned, then smiled, "I think you will be bored. Come along then," she stormed off the dais and down a side corridor.

The fat man wheezed, "Thank you."

"I suggest you take a break. You look like you are about to collapse from the heat," Mary laid a hand on his shoulder, "I'll see what I can do to help here."

***

An hour later Mary defended the entire council from the Queen. Carlith threw fire as easily as her words in temper.

Mary figured out why Carlith wielded so much fire.

Every time Carlith brought fire to her hand, an outline formed of the fire spirit. They were linked.

Mary worried the reason lava would consume everything lay in the heart of a fourteen year old girl.

Like Mary's curse set her on the path of villainess, young Carlith ran the path in glee. However Mary knew she did wrong. Carlith didn't seem to realize she rapidly became evil.

Mary watched Carlith growing angry again, so Mary used her words instead of magic this time, "So numerous fights broke out over water, water diverted to the volcano instead of the fountains, a dozen scouts along your border, drying farmland and livestock dying of thirst."

Carlith turned to Mary, summoning another fireball.

"You attack me, Queen Carlith, and you will see why I am a force to be reckoned with," Mary shifted her attention to the girl, "I am going to stop this catastrophe with your help, or without."

All the councilors pulled back, looking pale as Carlith shook.

"Queen Carlith, you are not letting your advisors advise. To tell you of the troubles in your land so you as ruler can deal with them, or summon someone like me to. If you rather we two fight each other to the death, I am willing to do so."

Carlith sulked, "Go ahead."

Mary looked at the councilors, "Did I cover all the issues?"

They nodded warily, all their eyes on their queen.

"Who stands to benefit from this?"

It drew all their eyes to her.

She sighed, "If there is a person or group behind this, they are doing it for a reason. Greed, love, hate, envy, rage and many other emotions drive people to action. What could be driving your enemy on this?"

"We joined your kingdoms when this started," the head councilor noted calmly.

"Is there a monetary benefit if you pull out of the Hundred and One Kingdoms?"

"No. It would weaken us further."

"Is there something of value here someone wants and be made available if this continues?"

"There are too many to list. Our magics come from alchemy and potions. We have sizable mines of gold, silver and iron. Our farmland is extensive when not tinder dry."

"Our queen," Sarith stated.

Mary looked at Carlith, nodded, "They could be targeting you, Queen Carlith."

"I will not be taken down," she sneered.

"Every mage has a breaking point. You can't fight off an army without exhausting yourself. All the fire you've thrown is wearing you down, Queen Carlith."

"And you can?"

"Even I tire. There are others whom reach their limit and need others to help them defeat villains."

She thought back to Gerard and his defeat at the hands of a vision.

"Councilors, would you put together a list of valuable assets? Queen Carlith, you should look it over and mark which ones you view as important."

"Me?"

"You are the ruler and know what is important. I would like to view the potions if I may. Perhaps one of the them is at the heart of this attack."

Carlith waved the councilors out, "Go. I will escort her to the library."

Once they were alone, Carlith considered Mary, each staring at the other.

"You would keep blocking me until we both died of exhaustion," Carlith said at the end.

"I'm a champion. I have to fight with all my strength to safeguard the people," just not the person she loved.

Carlith stood, "Our potion library is this way. You'll begin with the more dangerous books."

"That is a good point to start from, your Highness," Mary followed Carlith into the hall, "The more powerful the potion, the more likely the reason for this oppressive heat."

"You stood up to me," Carlith accused.

"I think everyone around you is too afraid to say no to you. If I hadn't stepped in, you would have injured or killed a couple dozen people. Do you want to follow that path?"

"This is the library, come with me. We'll look at the books together."

***

Three hours later Mary felt her eyes crossing. Potions for reviving trees, curing poisons, purifying water, earth and even lava. Turning the page she read about the vision potion.

A normal person could gain for a brief time the ability of a great seer.

She straighten, read further, noting the ingredients and instructions.

If she acted, she could see what Gerard had, know what fate moved against them.

Her heart raced until she turned away.

"Why does the vision potion interest you?"

Mary looked at Carlith, weighed the answers and choose the safest one, "A seer of great power sent me here, but he'll die if I succeed in defeating the evil rising. He is a dear friend and all I can think is being forewarned is to be prepared."

"This potion easily turns around and shows only the most horrible visions. The masters are careful in brewing it as too many students perished making it," Carlith touched the page, "My father drank a vision potion before he negotiated joining the hundred kingdoms. I wonder if he saw his death."

"Drank? It says in the book to pour it on earth."

"We keep some knowledge out of the books. If brewed correctly and poured into the river or fountains, it will grant visions of everyone's future spouse or children. If brewed incorrectly it shows all seers only ill fate."

Mary knew why Gerard saw only his death.

"How do you break such a wall of ill omen?" Mary asked, "It sounds like anyone could blind your seers."

She smiled, "All the seers of this city have a dose of the potion, brewed right. If they think they are being blinded, they drink the potion and see truly."

If only Mary could get a dose to Gerard, but she couldn't. Maybe his death could be averted.

"That sounds valuable. Blinding seers in all kingdoms would bring this sort of destruction," Mary scowled, "Why heat? Is your kingdom prone to severe weather like this?"

Carlith frowned, "No. We get a lot of rain and fields are green over half the year."

"Have you seen rain recently?"

Carlith got to her feet angrily, "I haven't set foot outside ever. I'm not allowed out of the palace."

Mary looked outside, noticed night arrived, "Why don't we rest, Queen Carlith. I think tomorrow will give us more answers to who plagues your city."

"The fields are burned, the livestock dead. Why would anyone die for this kingdom?" the girl turned and ran away.

Mary swore Carlith had tears in her eyes.

Sarith swept out of the stacks like a wraith, "I have prepared a room for you."

Mary didn't trust him after the smirk earlier, "I'll sleep with my horse. I'm used to the outdoors."

She left him scowling after her.

***

Waterfall whispered, "You think Gerard saw these terrible visions because of the potion?"

"Which means someone brewed the potion wrong to produce the ill fate visions. Possibly to blind all seers. I may be able to save him."

Waterfall pondered a moment then asked, "What if you are hoping when it isn't true?"

Mary snapped at Waterfall, "I won't let him die. Whoever did this will suffer."

"You don't sound like Lady Mary right now."

Mary covered her eyes, "Waterfall, I won't give up on him. I love him."

"If it's true."

"It's true."

Waterfall patiently continued, "If he is fated to die to save all the kingdoms including this one, what are you willing to sacrifice to avert his death? This kingdom? All of them?"

Tears threatened Mary but she refused to give in, "These visions tormenting him are a lie. He said it himself, he's never had a happy ending fail to occur as he saw."

"I prayed when I was captured my foals would get away, survive," Waterfall stated softly, "If the gods saved them, I'd suffer to the end of my days. The slaver who caught me showed me he caught my foals, that they would do their work to eat, or die. Everyday, a little bit of them faltered. I prayed until my last foal died, dragged behind the wagon I was yoked to. If I died, my foals would have lived because they couldn't pull the wagon, even chained together."

Mary looked up, "Good always wins."

"Sometimes the win is minor when we want a larger one," Waterfall looked over the courtyard, "I'll keep watch tonight. You have a long day ahead."

***

Mary woke from bad dreams, shivering.

She watched Gerard die in each one, lava keeping her from getting to him. Even her elemental failed her.

"Lady Mary?"

The horse master stood with the stable boy.

She stood, brushing hay from her clothes, "Yes?"

"I offer my services to you as part of my life debt. How may I help you?"

"I would like to know from your point of view, when did the heat and troubles come?"

"Six months ago when King Amerith was murdered. The volcano rumbled for a day and night. Then it calmed. A month ago the heat came. Never felt anything like it in thirty years. Does that help Lady Mary?"

"Did the volcano do the same thing when Amerith became king?"

The horse master scratched his head, "Yes. It did. Also for Queen Aslith before him. She only reigned for five years."

Mary rubbed her head, trying to figure out how this all fit in with the heat, the visions and Carlith.

"I need to ponder on what you have told me," she looked to Waterfall who twisted her head around the edge of her stall, "Would you be willing to walk Waterfall for an hour? I prefer she is kept in town in case I need her."

He looked nervously at Waterfall, "Certainly, Lady Mary."

Waterfall whinnied, acting like a regular horse.

Mary hoped Waterfall would hear something on the streets while she dealt with Carlith.

Mary finished righting her clothing, then walked into the palace.

Carlith sat on the throne, looking bored.

Only guards kept her company.

"Queen Carlith. I would like your opinion on a line of questioning."

Carlith swung her feet, "On what?"

"The fire spirit. Is it a valuable asset to your people?"

Carlith's lips trembled, then firmed, "In ancient times, the volcano would spew black ash to guard the capital against invaders."

"The water sent to drown the fire spirit might be an attempt to subdue it. To weaken it so it couldn't be summoned to aid."

"Only someone of the royal bloodline can command the fire spirit. Anyone else who attempts to will be killed by the spirit," Carlith stood, "The advisors gave me the list and I have my selections. Let's see what they say."

Mary walked with Carlith to the councilor's room, noticing the girl seemed calmer.

The councilors greeted Carlith warily.

"My queen, we looked over your marks and would like to discuss each of them in turn so we may end this swiftly," the head councilor bowed his head.

Mary listened to them speak about all the resources, why each was important to Barnarthi and to the surrounding kingdoms.

By agreement of the councilors and Carlith, they determined potions followed by the mines were the targets.

Mary thought otherwise.

If the enemy targeted the fire spirit, then they may be after Carlith, too. She had a connection to the fire spirit.

A connection her father took up when he became king.

Perhaps who ever did this wanted to snatch the control and then summon the lava. They lose control and Gerard...

Carlith suddenly stood, "I'm done here."

"My queen," the head councilor sounded like they weren't done.

She whirled and threw fire.

Mary extinguished the fire, but noticed it took longer to dissipate in her elemental.

Carlith grew stronger.

"I don't want to be stuck in this stuffy palace, talking every hour on issues other people should deal with," Carlith screamed at the councilor.

Mary remembered herself pounding at the magic barrier, screaming to be let out, to see her family. To escape her fate.

"Queen Carlith, why don't we look over the mines. The head councilor said they are all viewable within an afternoon."

Carlith gaped at Mary, eyes wide in shock.

"We can't risk the queen out there," Sarith argued, appearing behind Carlith.

"Queen Carlith, why don't we ride out and see the mines, just like we reviewed the potions. We can determine if they are targets or reasons for the attacks."

"Yes. Sarith have my horse readied," Carlith ordered.

Mary admitted she enjoyed his anger. She felt his frustrations made up partially for the smirk earlier.

In less than half an hour, Mary rode Waterfall beside Carlith. Mary looked back, noted two guards discretely following them through the crowd.

Mary watched the crowds form a wide berth around Carlith, their heads bowed.

They obviously feared their queen. Considering how easily Carlith used fire, Mary didn't blame them.

When they cleared the city walls, Carlith looked around in curiosity.

Like the child she appeared to be.

The guards lost their cover but they stayed with Carlith and Mary.

"What do you think of your kingdom, Queen Carlith?"

"I love being outside. I always wanted to adventure like my father did in his youth," Carlith kicked her horse and they bolted down the road.

Mary smiled, nudged Waterfall to follow.

The guards struggled to keep up as Mary paced Carlith.

The girl smiled, laughing.

Too quickly they arrived at the first mine.

"Do I have to do this?" Carlith whined.

"I ask myself that quite often."

"You? The champion who stopped a vampire from slaying the lizard king? The woman who restored the leystone mines? Why would you say that?"

"Did they tell you the story of how I became a champion?"

"No."

Mary sighed, "I owe a debt to every kingdom in the original hundred. To remove these debts I must act as champion. I am sent after large troubles, and tend to pick up smaller ones on the way, all needing fixes."

"What keeps you going?"

"That seer I told you about? He saved me from death, because he originally saw me holding a child."

"Originally?" Carlith stopped her horse.

"He's seen terrible events unfolding. Events which will kill the man I am to marry and bear children for."

"That's why you stopped on the vision potion. You wanted to see what he did."

Mary nodded, looked at Carlith, "His sense of duty is stronger than mine. I pay my debts to get to my future husband. He does it for the good of everyone."

"He sent you here," Carlith swallowed, "What is going to happen?"

"If I had not arrived, lava would destroy most of the kingdoms, kill the seer, and leave me to lead the survivors, though I will bear children, just not with the man who was to be my husband. Since I am here, the seer will die to stop an evil from taking control of your kingdom. I will live on to have a child, again not with my husband."

Carlith asked, "Perhaps that is why my father is dead. He saw there were two paths to take."

"Let's do what we can with what tools we do have. I, for one, want to find this enemy and make sure this kingdom is safe. In doing so maybe my friend will live, and I will be with my husband."

"You have a happy ending ahead of you. What do I have? Cooped up in this kingdom to only speak."

Mary struck on an idea, something to help get Carlith out and about, yet assist her people, "Have you thought of being your kingdom's champion?"

"What?"

"You could adventure, albeit only within your kingdom. You'd need to have your magic under control, a bit of training, but you could defend this kingdom as your father did."

Carlith engrossed herself into reviewing the mine, her smile relaxing the miners.

Mary hoped Carlith would repay her blood debts faster than Mary.

They returned to the city, discussing what they saw, and what they didn't find.

No sign of the enemy at work.

They dismounted, the two guards riding in after them.

Mary saw the Speaker of the Fairies hovering at the top of the stairs, her eyes glittering malevolently.

Carlith huffed, "I suppose we have to meet."

"We do. The fairies are the nearest kingdom to your south. You should leave us," the fairy sneered the last at Mary.

Mary bowed, "As you wish, Speaker of the Fairies."

Leading Waterfall, Mary retired to the stable.

The stable boy waited for her, with a meal he wanted to share.

When she asked why, and got his answer, she glared at Waterfall who looked innocent.

Waterfall gave the stable boy and his friends rides around the city.

***

Mary dozed, thinking of what else she could do to help Carlith away from her path.

Her dream showed Carlith throwing out fire, the fire spirit empowering her. Mary faced her, her water elemental barely holding back Carlith's assault.

Then Sarith rose behind Carlith, a dagger plunging toward her back.

An earth elemental slammed into him, sending him into a wall.

Carlith saw him collapse then turned her fire on Gerard who stood in the entrance, King Silva beside him.

Mary jerked upright, covering her mouth in horror, the burnt stench of Gerard's death clogging her nose.

The stable boy stood before her, looking upset.

"What is it?" she managed to whisper.

"I'm sorry. I gave you the potion my mother had. It was made long ago."

"Potion?" she frowned.

"You said to Waterfall you wished you could stop a death foreseen by a seer. I gave you my mother's vision potion last night."

Mary opened her mouth to ask him why, when a scream jerked her head up.

The Speaker of Fairies shot out of the palace, her guards forming around her.

Flames burst out after her, but couldn't catch her.

Mary ran inside, Waterfall charging beside her.

Guards ran everywhere, shouting in confusion.

When she gained the throne room she found Catlith wreathed in flames.

"You," she pointed at Mary, "You pretended to be my friend, Siren."

Mary's elemental barely covered her in time. Steam billowed from where the elemental meet fire, forcing Waterfall to retreat out of the room.

"Queen Carlith, what do you mean? I'm a champion of the Hundred and One Kingdoms. I'm trying to save your kingdom."

"The Speaker of the Fairies said you killed hundreds of champions. Sarith said you must have sent the water against us."

Mary cursed the Speaker. If she kept her mouth shut, then Carlith wouldn't be fighting her now.

"I didn't send the water against you. I only want to stop the lava from destroying the Hundred and One Kingdoms," even if it killed Gerard.

The fire grew more potent, pushing Mary back so her water elemental could fill more space.

"You will do anything to save the seer. Even kill me. Sarith said so."

"What?" Mary kept her focus on her elemental as it wanted to leave. It didn't like the fire and began to fight her to flee.

Then like in her vision, Sarith rose up behind Carlith, his knife going for her back.

"Carlith, behind you!" Mary tried to warn, fighting to keep her elemental between her and Carlith.

Carlith turned in time to see Sarith get smashed backwards by an earth elemental.

Mary turned her head and saw Gerard just like the vision. He looked resigned to his fate as he turned to face Carlith. It broke her heart to see him so vulnerable and unwilling to see another way to end this.

Silva's frill extended as he looked worried. He still summoned his fire, determined to face the danger.

His fire magic wouldn't help him. Carlith was too powerful.

Mary knew she had only one way to save Gerard.

She flung her elemental over Gerard, knowing Carlith would burn her instead.

Gerard yelled, "Mary!"

She closed her eyes, the flame coming toward her, "Goodbye, my love."

She expected searing pain, but there was only heat and light.

Peeking, she watched the fire turn to smoke, then clear.

Carlith sobbed, "Why did my father do it?"

She collapsed, holding herself tight enough to whiten her knuckles.

Mary cautiously walked to the crying girl, "What did he do?"

"My uncle, he tried to kill me, but father dove in front of me. Why did my father do it?"

Mary knelt, understanding a man she never met, "Because he loved you. When you love someone, you are willing to die to protect them."

Carlith blinked back tears, "He should have lived. I'm not half the ruler he was."

"He died so you could rule. He saw signs you were to be the next ruler. He started your training, right?"

"He took me into the volcano," she clung to Mary, "He said the fire spirit chooses the next ruler. I was so afraid when I saw it, I ran away."

"You recognized its power and how much responsibility it meant."

"It can destroy everything. How could I be expected to control it, to sooth it?"

"The connection goes both ways," Mary sensed the spell beneath her, subtler than before.

Water redirected against the fire spirit again.

Mary severed it violently as she stood, hugging the crying girl.

Sarith groaned, his helm falling free of his head.

He had the same colored hair as Carlith.

It made sense then. Sarith's smirk earlier, letting Carlith kill everyone around her, and finally trying to kill Carlith.

"So Sarith, you are also of the bloodline. That's why you egged Carlith to attack me. You wanted her dead by my hands. I bet King Amerith trusted you. You gave him a badly brewed vision potion so he saw only two vile futures. Then you poured another to block the visions of all seers."

"It only blocked visions of this kingdom. We saw Gerard's kingdom crumbling without him," Silva hissed.

Carlith stared at her guard in horror, "You gave my father bad visions?"

He stood, his sneer mirrored in the water elemental he summoned, "I am the rightful heir to the throne."

Carlith screamed, "How could you kill my father!"

Mary held her, "Don't Carlith. He intended to harm all the kingdoms."

"My father!"

"He's killed more people than that. He intentionally allowed you to strike anyone who you didn't like and probably eliminated anyone who tried to straighten this out."

Sarith snapped, "You who's killed every champion sent against you."

"I knew I would pay the price for those deaths one day, Sarith. I thought I'd be killed for my actions, but instead I am paying my debts by standing in the place of those I murdered," Mary explained as she looked for his spell.

His elemental rushed forward, but Mary foresaw that.

She knew the feel of his magic so she broke his spell over the elemental the instant she found it.

The elemental stopped, towering over her and Carlith for a few seconds then rushed back at Sarith.

His scream cut off swiftly as the water elemental changed to crimson.

Mary sent the water elemental away so it wouldn't cause more harm, "Your father has been avenged."

"I thought he was my guardian angel. He always helped me."

"He hid so he could strike from behind. He knew seers are a big asset for the Hundred and One Kingdoms so he blinded them from seeing the best route," she looked at Gerard, "So we had to choose the best of two bad paths."

Gerard sat down, "The visions."

Silva snorted, "It may have blocked visions of this kingdom, but my seers saw Gerard dying here when an obscured path led to him living," Silva scowled, "We've worked on a spell to empower the seers so we wouldn't be blinded again like with the black dragon. It partially cleared the vision."

Waterfall cautiously walked into the throne room, her eyes scanning for fire, before rubbing her head on Mary's shoulder.

Mary muttered, "He should have thought his visions obscured rather than to sacrifice himself."

Carlith looked at Gerard then up at Mary, her eyes wide, as she whispered, "He's the seer you were trying to save?"

"Yes," Mary walked over to a chair, slumped into it, "Your stable boy gave my a vision potion with the meal we shared last night. I saw you burning Gerard to death as I tried to defend myself. When I saw us going down that path, I couldn't let you kill him. I rather die than let him perish."

Waterfall trotted over to Mary, "I'm sorry. I couldn't help you."

Mary patted the kelpie's nose, "It's okay. Fire is your weakness. I seriously thought I would die."

"I'm sorry," Carlith sniffed, "I was so furious once I heard what the Speaker of the Fairies said about you."

"I think I killed someone close to her when I fought on the other side. I doubt my debts to her kingdom will ever be paid," Mary looked at the young Queen, "You'll need to practice your politics. You are entering an ocean of them."

"I would have killed you before you got with your husband."

Gerard looked over, "You told her of the vision?"

"You have no right to use that tone with me," Mary stood and stormed to him, "You gave up. You couldn't see the vision anymore so you didn't fight it. Didn't choose to believe in me."

Her finger jabbed him in the chest, "You gave me back my life, set me on the path to being good. Then you abandoned me because you couldn't think of another reason for you losing the vision."

Silva asked, "What vision would be strong enough to make you fight so hard, Mary?"

Mary glared at him, "Stay out of this."

Gerard sighed, "I saw her husband and her child."

Silva considered Mary, "I pity the man who ends up tied to you."

"Pity Gerard should he give up on me again," Mary turned to Waterfall, "Let's go. These two kings should be able to handle the situation from here. Considering they didn't think to tell me the whole truth from the beginning."

She stomped to the stable and helped the stable boy ready Waterfall for a ride.

"Lady Mary, please wait," Carlith pleaded.

Mary turned to the queen.

"I rather you stayed until I can be my kingdom's champion. I need someone to save me from myself, for now."

Mary smiled, "Did those two encourage this?"

"I gave a vision potion to King Gerard so he could see clearly and he said I need your calm to help me until I can stand on my own. I don't want to kill people but I'm still not ready to be queen."

The old Gerard returned, so Mary replied, "I suppose I could stay."

"My queen!" A haggard man rushed into the courtyard, "A terrible beast is savaging my village. Please help us."

Mary looked up to the two kings standing at the top of the stairs.

"Well, Queen Carlith. It seems your champion training will begin today. Let's ride."

Mary and Carlith thundered out of the city, both better than before.

Part V

Siren's Song

Mary fought a scowl as she watched the crowd swarm the newly available prince.

She leaned against a pillar, watching the mothers and daughters all fighting to get even a second of the prince's attention.

Rubbing the last piece of jewelry she wore, she wondered if Gerard sent her here to keep from murdering a certain fairy.

"Rubbing your earring won't make it go away," a familiar voice scattered her thoughts.

She turned to Silva, king of the lizards, and smiled, "Neither will standing here looking pretty, like you."

Silva wore more ornaments than she'd seen him in. His frill couldn't be seen for all the gold and silver wrapped over it. He wore a chain mesh over his head highlighting his smooth scalp and the wealth he commanded. His muted red skin gleamed as if he shed recently.

"I imagine you rather be out killing a certain troublemaker," he stood beside her, towering her six foot frame easily.

They watched the constantly shifting group in front of them for a long while, their silence companionable.

Mary frowned as she revisited her prior thoughts, "They don't swarm him like this."

"Swarm who?"

She looked up at Silva, "I've never seen women nor girls do this to King Gerard. I've seen this behavior at three coming out galas but never seen it with Gerard."

"No one told you the tale?"

"What tale?" She huffed, "Most people only look at me long enough to beg for help, or to run away."

"Have your heard of the Snow Witch?"

"Something about avoiding Chillwind Peak. Just tell me the tale."

"No one knows how she came to be upon Chillwind Peak, but the first encounter was with a young bard who wanted to get a feather for his cap. He climbed the tallest peak to see if he could capture a wind spirit. Instead he ran into the Snow Witch. She kept him for seven days and seven nights, imprisoned for her pleasure."

Mary did not want to hear about such an encounter with Gerard, "Did she kill him?"

"No, something far worse. She took his manhood."

She whirled to Silva alarmed, "Literally?"

His frill flared out, settled, "Magically, she stole his seed. She released him to return to the kingdoms with a warning. All men who enter her domain will be unable to sow their seed."

"Of course Gerard would go after her," Mary growled.

How could Gerard be her future husband if he couldn't perform.

"He wasn't the first champion to try, nor the last. We get at least one champion a year foolishly going against her and returns half a man. Gerard escaped before the seventh day with the help of the fairies when they collected one of their own. The seers say a man would defeat her one day, which encourages every young man to go up there."

"Have any women champions gone up against her?"

"We have so few and they have no interest in fighting something unbeatable by a woman."

Mary smiled as a thought struck her, "They saw a man fight her. What if the champion only looked like a man?"

Silva looked at her with a brow raised, "Do go on."

"It's a distant possibility, but what if I went after the Snow Witch? I'm a powerful mage, and I can get something crafted to contain leystones. With the right dressing and a regular horse, I could look like a man."

"Or you could come back infertile. How would your future husband think of that?"

He's already infertile so we'll make a perfect pair, she thought darkly.

"It will take time to set this up. I'll need a blacksmith for armor and a sword. Leystones to enable me to overpower the Snow Witch."

"A horse, not a kelpie. You are well known. If you ride up without a banner or some symbol of a kingdom she'll smell a trap."

"I need a seamstress," she looked up at him, "and a place to set this all up."

Silva smiled, "I suppose my cave will do?"

"Oh yes," she grinned, "I think it's time for me to take on this scourge."

***

The next day she sent out messengers to her conspirators.

The Stonesieges to bring material for her armor and sword. They would hopefully bring a couple leystones she could borrow for this adventure from the family who owned the mine.

The boy she saved from highwaymen had become quite skilled since she last saw him. He'd paid his dues and grown well known for his craft, black smithing.

Another note went to Queen Carlith to summon the horse master of her kingdom with a steed worthy of a champion.

The seamstress would be told of the plan when Silva and Mary arrived.

She escorted Silva back to his kingdom, thinking of everything she should also prepare.

A fancy saddlebag, clothes made of expensive fabric, helmet to cover her face.

"Are you sure you don't want to include Gerard?"

She felt a twinge of pain in her chest, "I'm sure. I'm doing this. I defeat her and I give him back his life."

"You don't trust his vision will be true?"

"I'm worried I am going the wrong way, but I don't want to risk him. If I take him, she may keep him. If I lose my fertility, I'll still have him."

Silva hummed, "Ah, so I was right."

"Right about what?"

"I wondered why Gerard spared you. You're meant to be his wife."

She flushed, uncomfortable with his gaze, "We'll see."

"That is why he had to be the one to go to your tower. Why he was willing to die to protect you."

"Silva, you shut it now or I will shove a rag in your mouth."

Waterfall looked up at her, "That's why you threw your elemental in front of him?"

"I thought you weren't talking to me since I'm going after the Snow Witch without you," Mary groused.

"I am still upset about that, but you are doing this for your true love."

Mary clutched the saddle as Waterfall shook excitedly.

"Stop that at once," Mary ordered.

By the time they arrived at Silva's palace, Waterfall unmercifully teased Mary to the point she wanted to strangle the kelpie.

Silva alleviated the tension by taking her to the seamstress.

"Lady Mary, it is a pleasure to see you again," the seamstress bowed her head.

"I am glad to see you as well. I have a special task which requires your skills. You'll be working with a blacksmith, dwarves and a horse master to put together a disguise."

"A disguise?"

Mary explained her plan and what she needed to put it together.

"I can once I know the colors and metals to be used," the seamstress took out a length of string, "I will measure so we have ideas to work with. You will need something to run and fight in, but look like a prince."

"I have money for the fabrics," Mary offered.

"I will pay for this part," Silva stated, "I can't fight beside you like with the vampire. I'll host the ones making your armor and disguise."

"I will pay you back."

"Defeat this particular trouble and I would think us even. Quite a few will look at me in respect for hosting the one who took down the Snow Witch. I imagine my seamstress will be in great demand."

Mary grinned, "The blacksmith, the horse master, the Stonesieges and those children, too."

"This will take time to make," the seamstress commented as she moved around Mary, "Many components, care needed for clothing, cloak, boots so give appearance of prince champion."

"How long would you expect?"

"A couple months."

Mary nodded, "For a fine disguise the Snow Witch will take at first glance, that is acceptable."

Silva added, "You'll be traveling by horse and not kelpie. You'll take a month to get there from here since you can't ride the rivers. We should plan your route so you arrive in the best time."

The next two weeks went by in a blur as each of her allies arrived, brought up to speed and then did their measurements and add their opinions.

They all decided steel chest plate and chain mail for arms and thighs. Gold and silver would be used for embellishments in the form of a fire spirit. The horse master said no one from his kingdom travelled far yet, so the kingdom's emblem would not be immediately recognized by the Snow Witch.

They measured Mary ten different times so they could work without her for a few weeks.

Silva joined her in the courtyard of his palace as she spoke with Waterfall.

"I am not certain you should answer this missive," he started before he handed it over.

Mary read the letter, shocked the fairies called for her aid.

"This is unexpected. Why after months of refusing my aid or sending their own champions, would they ask for me? Their Speaker hates me."

Silva's frill flared, "A trap no doubt."

"They say if I don't come, my debt will be doubled," Mary growled, "I have to go. I don't want this ring to get bigger."

Waterfall looked over the paper, "You may be able to turn this to clearing your debt."

Mary looked up at the room her friends and allies worked at her costume.

"Go on. I'll make sure they keep at it. See if you can finally clear your debt with the fairy kingdom."

She smiled at Silva, "Thank you, King Silva. I'll be back as soon as I can so we can deal with the Snow Witch.

His stable hands readied Waterfall and filled her saddlebags with supplies.

Mary rode out, hoping she could clear her final debt.

***

Mary expected to be delayed from entering the kingdom or forced to wait days for an audience with the Speaker of the Fairies.

When a guard escorted her in immediately, she felt trepidation.

The Speaker sat on a swing dangling from the ceiling, her face imperious and distant.

Mary knelt, "Speaker of the Fairies."

"The King wished you summoned for a task to begin paying your debt," The Speaker stated, "Our champions have already been sent. If you succeed in defeating this monster we'll consider half your debt paid."

Mary kept her suspicions out of her tone and voice, "I would gladly take up this quest. May I know where I should start on the trail of this monster?"

A commotion sounded behind Mary and then a large head thudded beside her.

The head came from a dire wolf three times the largest size she'd heard about.

"It seems you did not complete this quest before my people killed it. Your debt is doubled," The Speaker smiled down at Mary.

Mary barely felt the increase in weight as her fury surged.

Instead of lashing out as she might have under other circumstances, Mary bowed her head, "As you have no need of my services, I will continue on my other quest."

She stood, turned and marched out of the hall.

In the courtyard she whistled for Waterfall since Mary didn't see her anywhere.

"Are you going after the beast?"

Mary turned to a peasant dressed male fairy standing on a branch equal to her eyes.

"The beast is already dead. I will be leaving and never setting foot on this land again."

He looked shocked, "Why is that?"

She shook her head, "I have tried to help this kingdom. Any time I heard of a danger I sent word I was willing to stand with the fairies. Every time I was told fairy champions would deal with it. This is the first time I've been summoned here and the instant I accept the quest, the head of the beast is delivered. My debt is now doubled. Next time you call for aid, I will give serious thought to not answering."

She strode down the steps as Waterfall arrive, festooned with dozens of fairy children.

Sighing, Mary said calmly, "Sorry, young ones. Waterfall and I have a quest. Play time is over."

The chorus of disappointed whines sank Mary's hopes to depart quickly.

"Alright, once around the city. Then I have to go."

Mary sat on the ground as Waterfall tore off to the delighted squeals from the children.

She thought on what she needed for the Snow Witch quest.

If she attempted to prepare any spells ahead of time, the Snow Witch would sense it upon approach. Her water elemental had to be kept small so as not to arouse suspicion.

Something flitted in front of her face.

She looked up at the peasant who hovered at eye level.

"I asked a question but you did not hear."

"I don't answer to you or any fairy," she stated coldly, "You rather have Siren under leash, than to reward Lady Mary. If I die with this debt, I will gladly take it than to suffer the humiliation your people want to visit on me until the end of time. Now leave me alone so I can prepare for a quest worthy of Lady Mary."

She closed her eyes and ignored the fairy.

Mary forgot to mention barding to the seamstress for the horse. The chill up there would hurt the mount. She didn't need it with Waterfall. The kelpie could go just about anywhere with little issue and only needed water to keep going.

If she succeeded, Gerard may be livid with her. She knew it would hurt, but she did this for him. To free him from the curse and let them be together.

What name should she give the child?

Shaking her head at the thought, she opened her eyes.

To the peasant sitting out of reach staring at her.

"What is it? You get pleasure out of staring at the captive Siren?" she sneered.

"I wonder why you say such things."

She stood, "Ask the Speaker. She's the one that torments me still. I proved myself willing to lay down my life to protect the kingdoms. Are you?"

She strode out of the courtyard, whistling to let Waterfall know she walked to the city wall.

Away from the hellish pit.

***

Mary leaned outside the walls, looking at the sky when Waterfall rejoined her.

"Why didn't you stay in the courtyard? It had shade."

"A pesky fairy asking question he should already know the answer to if he dared to looked beyond prejudice. Let's go. I want to get on with my quests."

She almost leapt into the saddle, eager to leave the cursed land of fairies behind.

Waterfall trotted out immediately, her ears twitching as she thought.

"What bee is in your ear now?" Mary asked an hour later.

"I saw your debt earring is twice the size it was. What happened with the Speaker?"

"She charged me with a quest her champions already completed, but not delivered the proof," Mary knew the Speaker set it up that way, "She knew when I crossed into their lands and probably sent everything against the huge dire wolf. The head could have swallowed your chest easily. Then she doubled my debt for failing to complete the quest before her champions."

"You didn't kill her?" Waterfall stopped and looked up at Mary, "That is astonishing."

"Not worth the effort. She'd be replaced by another hateful fairy to hold my shackles. I wish to return to Silva quickly. Might as well get his snickers out of the way."

It took them a week to return as it seemed every minor quest along the way slowed Mary.

Mary clomped into the palace, carrying her mood as a storm.

Silva took one look at her ear, then her face, turned back to the seamstress, "Let's proceed with your idea now Lady Mary has returned."

"I look forward to good news," Mary growled then sat down.

"I asked for a wig maker to craft you a disguise for your hair. However, he says you need to cut your hair so it fits properly."

She picked up a strand and considered it. She hadn't cut her hair except to get out tough snags. Mary sighed in defeat. She'd do anything to accomplish this.

"Cut away. Make me bald if you need to. I don't want this Snow Witch to have a single inkling I'm not as seen."

"You should also practice a swagger like a man."

Huffing out a breath Mary nodded, "True. I'll start today. No comment from you," she pointed a finger at Silva whose frill shook with his amusement.

"I wouldn't dare."

***

Two months passed and she finalized her disguise.

She'd trained with the horse when she wasn't talking and walking like a man.

A warhorse, he took her weight easily even when she donned the practice armor. She knew the commands to make him charge, trample and rear but she hoped she never needed them.

The dwarves and the blacksmith strode out, carrying bundles with them, as she brushed down her mount, considering the fight ahead.

"My lady," The blacksmith bowed, "I wish to present you your armor and weapons."

She nodded, turned to face them.

He pulled a cloth off the first bundle.

"This is steel plate, embossed with the symbol of the fire spirit. Gold and silver trim along with rubies to hide the fact you wear four leystones worked into the metal. The chain mail is attached underneath the shoulder so if you need, you can loosen it and get free. The leggings are not as easy to free, but can be managed. The gauntlets are made of steel, also embellished with the fire spirit. No spikes per your request," he pulled off the cover of the next bundle, "Leather boots, trimmed in gold and silver thread, sporting the house of Levitten. They are servants to Queen Carlith and once fielded knights for her family. The doublet adds padding and hides your figure. It is embellished with the fire spirit and the crest of Levitten."

He took the last bundle and unwrapped it.

"This is your sword. I made it more like a saber to give you heft and, if you can use your horse's momentum, to slice through without breaking the blade. Hilt is gilded in gold and silver to give it the same feel as the armor."

She drew the sword, tried a couple practice swings, "This will do."

"The seamstress made this cloak so it shows the same two emblems as the doublet," he unfolded the cloak, "It matches the barding created for your horse."

"I doubt the Snow Witch will see through this."

"She won't," the dwarf snorted, "Why don't we get you ready to ride out."

She nodded, "About time. She's dead as soon as I get there."

At least this she could do. She would succeed in defeating an enemy who took away a man's ability to seed children. Not like the stupid fairy quest.

"Is everything else ready to go?" Mary asked.

"Silva says for you go on up,"

She stalked into the palace and went in search of Silva.

He stood with the seamstress.

"We'll have to cut your hair now, Lady Mary," Silva stated, "then weave the wig into the remaining hair to hold it in place while you journey to Chillwind Peak."

She sat in the chair he offered, "Do it. I'm eager to get started."

Each snip made her think of her hair and how she'd kept it through her imprisonment, her villainess days, and her quests.

She hoped Gerard wouldn't care about her hair, despite what his vision showed.

"Did you want to see your hair before we do the weave?" The seamstress asked.

"No. I'll see the result once you're done."

It felt weird having claws pulling and yanking on her hair, brushing her scalp.

She remembered her mother brushing her hair so long ago, how she tangled her hair so badly her mother brushed it for an hour just to set it right. This felt like that.

"My lady, we are done."

Mary opened her eyes and gaze at herself in the mirror. The blond hair lay straight to just under her ears. It made her look like an innocent prince.

"We would like to apply this too," the seamstress held out a strip of something the same color as her new hair.

"Won't a fake beard come off?" She looked up.

"Not with this glue," she patted a sealed jar, "We will color your eyebrows with ink. It'll take a couple months to wash out."

Mary blew out a breath, "I've come this far might as well do it right. Color my eyebrows and beard me."

She closed her eyes as they glued the beard and changed her eyebrow color.

"That is amazing," the horse master whistled, "I swear a man is sitting there."

"My seamstress and the wig maker are quite clever. I would be surprised if the Snow Witch could see the truth," Silva remarked, "With the armor, clothing and horse, she'll take the stage well."

"What about her name. She can't just go up there saying she's Lady Mary."

"How about Lord Malio?" The seamstress offered.

"From my kingdom? It would have to be Malith," the horse master replied.

"Done, my lady," the seamstress stated.

Mary blinked at her mirror self and admitted the medium length beard and eyebrow color made her look very manly.

"I think Malith is a good compromise," she stood, shook her head, testing the weave.

It stayed in place.

"Well, my lord Malith," Silva chuckled, "Let's get you off on your quest."

An hour later she strode through the halls, her armor and sword secured.

Lizards she knew well looked at her in confusion before ignoring her.

She came out to find Waterfall looking over her horse.

"Greetings, Waterfall," Mary enjoyed how her kelpie friend jumped, "Is something interesting with my steed, Valirith?"

Waterfall stared then cocked her head, "Lady Mary?"

Mary grinned, "Perhaps a few hours ago," she swept a bow, "I am Lord Malith."

Waterfall's head drooped, "I can't go with you."

Mary patted her friends head, "I wish you could, but you're too magical to disguise. I can hide long enough to draw her in."

"Please be safe. Don't cross the Red River turning a full moon. The eels are not friendly."

Mary laughed as she got into the saddle of her horse, "I will keep that in mind. Don't spoil the children while I'm away."

With a smile she left her friends behind.

***

A month later Mary wanted the stupid quest over with.

Her hair itched like crazy from bugs. She swept them out with her magic every few days just to gain some peace.

The beard caught food and she had to wipe down after every meal.

Valirith, her horse couldn't go as long as Waterfall, making Mary walk often or rest longer than she desired.

When the wind howled coldly by her and she finally saw the peak she sought, she wanted to cheer.

She paused at the start of the trail wandering up to the top, pulled out her banner.

The fire spirit blazed in vibrant red and gold thread on it as she secured it to her pole.

"Alright, Valirith. Let's show these cowardly kingdoms how we deal with witches," Mary smirked up at the peak.

Riding slowly up the trail, Mary keep an eye out for the Snow Witch.

She grew more tense the higher she rode.

Most stories said her quarry appeared long before the halfway point, and she passed that quickly with no sign of the Snow Witch.

Mary came around a bend and saw the land laid out below her. She'd reached the peak.

Angry the stupid witch hadn't shown, she slammed her banner into the snow, "I call this Snow Witch nothing more than a story!"

"I figured you would come all the way to the top."

Mary whirled Valirith to the speaker, her sword in her hand.

The pale figure looked to be snowflakes and ice made flesh.

The woman definitely made Mary feel really ugly, until she remembered she wore a disguise. Her enemy revealed an hourglass shape through nearly translucent cloth.

"I see you expected a beast," the Snow Witch purred, slowly stalking forward.

Mary felt the curse from the Snow Witch.

The Snow Witch didn't curse others, she was under the curse.

She would take in the seed of the men she seduced, stealing their warmth and giving them part of her curse.

Mary saw thousands of strands coming from the Snow Witch, floating outwards.

If the curse laid on a normal person, the sheer number of strands would have broken the woman free by now. However, the woman beneath the curse possessed power. Lots of it.

Mary cursed, "So you are just another victim."

The Snow Witch pulled back, "What do you mean?"

Mary summoned her elemental, picking up the snow from the ground and swirling it with the snow falling from the sky.

Mary charged at the woman, hoping the witch would cast a spell to stop her mount.

Instead the witch threw an earth elemental at Mary's water elemental, both clawing at each other as they tumbled.

Then Mary went flying, her horse skidding on his side.

She rolled, regaining her feet.

The Snow Witch grabbed her hand, pulled her close, "I will enjoy you in my cave. I am so cold and you are warm."

The curse reached out to cling to Mary, but snapped back as it couldn't settle in. Being female, Mary couldn't be added to the curse.

"No," Mary stated then slammed her head into the witch's face.

The witch howled, stumbling backwards.

Mary tapped three of the leystones and summoned a fireball.

She threw it at the witch who shielded with ice. The ice steamed.

"How dare you!" the witch shrieked, "I am the perfect woman!"

Mary smirked, advancing on the witch, "Nope. Only a cursed one."

The temperature dropped, the wind screaming by as the witch poured her magic into defense.

Ice spikes formed, shooting out past Mary's side, tearing her cloak.

"That cloak came from a better woman than you!" Mary taunted.

With a banshee cry, the witch stopped her shield spell, discarding magic then lunged at Mary.

Mary used her hilt to knock the witch aside, seeing the strands pulling away from the core of the curse.

"Queen Carlith shines with more heart and power than you!" Mary dodged a flung icicle, "Even Speaker of the Fairies is stronger."

A howl of rage preceded the witch flinging out a wall of snow, knocking Mary off her feet.

She tumbled over and over, losing track of where sky and ground were, surrounded by white. When the world stopped twirling, Mary stared upward, gasping for breath.

"I am the most beautiful and perfect woman in the world. No one can best me," the voice seemed to come from everywhere.

Mary struggled, fighting the snow but she couldn't break free.

Cold began sapping her strength until she lay exhausted in a hollow.

Then the Snow Witch straddled her.

"I will show you why all men love me."

Mary's anger drew everything and exploded outward, sending the witch flying.

Mary stood, panting, "They didn't love you. None of them. Gerard is mine."

The witch gaped, her pale cheeks glowing rosy as the curse cracked, "But you're a man."

Mary strode towards her, glaring down at the witch, "Gerard is mine to love and be loved by. You are nothing but a curse which lasted too long."

The witch scrambled to her feet, "You are mine. All of you are."

Mary stopped in front of the witch, looked down on her, "Darling, you don't own me," Mary leaned down, keeping the witch's attention on her face and not her hands, "For I'm a woman."

The witch gasped.

Mary thrust her magic into the cracks of the curse and shattered its anchor.

The strands whipped around them, making the witch scream in pain.

Mary caught her frail body as it convulsed.

When the last strand left, the snow witch lay naked, her skin turning to dark brown, her hair from white to black.

Mary told her elemental to help up the warhorse who was half buried in the snow, while she wrapped the woman on her cloak.

She carefully mounted the warhorse, noting the barding hung ragged in many places.

"Alright, time for Lord Malith to retire and Lady Mary to get home," Mary clucked to the horse to start down the trail.

***

Mary stopped at the first town, purchased clothes for the lady she rescued.

Miss Dalia was a potential mage but she gave it up to marry her sweetheart. Said sweetheart though had an affair with a real witch.

When the witch found out about Dalia, she cursed Dalia to attract men, ensnare them, then steal their manhood. Ever since Dalia lived at Chillwind Peak.

That started fifty years ago.

Dalia rode Valirith once she recovered. They all travelled back towards Silva's kingdom.

Mary dealt with minor troubles as she passed through, delaying her so she reached the halfway point after a month.

Her beard clung stubbornly as did the wig. Mary alternated between praising the tenacity of her disguise and detesting the discomfort.

"You could drop me at any village and race back to your Gerard," Dalia said as they reached the Red River and Mary found out the ferrymen wouldn't cross at night.

"I can't race to him. If I tried to, Waterfall would hunt me down, and one does not piss off a kelpie," Mary sighed as she considered the alternate paths, "Besides, I am not letting a mage potential of your power out of sight until we get you to a proper teacher or guild."

"My power?"

Mary looked up at Dalia, "The curse should have ended after about five years. It lasted fifty years since it drew from your innate power. You kept the spell running and easily could maintain it for another fifty years had I not come along."

Sighing, Mary headed to the nearest town, "We'll wait out the full moon. Then I think the guild on the border of King Silva's kingdom will welcome you."

Mary worried the beard and wig may become permanent. She wanted free of them and to see if she retained any hair to be vain about. Plus, get rid of the bugs.

They spent the night at an inn, waiting with dozens of nobles for the full moon to pass.

Mary listened to them talking, apparently all rushing to snag a king for their daughters or themselves.

She pitied the king forced to suffer their atrocious greed and ambition, or the empty-headiness of the daughters.

They departed the next morning and travel went faster.

Mary stopped at the guild tower and made sure they accepted Dalia, though she had to do it as Lord Malith and not Lady Mary.

Nearly three months after she set out, she rode up to the city gate. She yearned for her disguise to be removed and get a nice bath.

The guard on duty looked at her, his frill flaring in amusement, "Lord Malith. King Silva is waiting for you."

She raised an eyebrow, "Glad to hear that. I look forward to good news."

A celebration crowded the streets, forcing her to dismount and walk her horse through.

She gained the palace courtyard, exhausted and foot weary.

"You did it," Waterfall nuzzled her so hard Mary stumbled.

"I did?" Mary yawned.

Silva chuckled, "Ten of my champions long infertile are free of the Snow Witch's curse. That is why you braved the crowds today."

"All I want is this damnable beard, and wig off, then a nice bath. I hope you can arrange it," she leaned against Waterfall, "Lord Malith retires."

***

126

It took two days to remove the beard and wig, both being stuck fast to her.

When her face looked like her own, only with very short hair, she thanked her allies, returning the armor, leystones and all, to the dwarves, and the horse to the horse master.

The seamstress laughed at the tattered barding and cloak, though she found the banner flying at Chillwind Peak more amusing.

Silva escorted Mary to the borders of his land as she rode to Gerard.

"I've heard Gerard is swamped with women," he said as they paused at his border.

"What?"

"He's fertile again."

Mary scowled, "I would have taken off immediately if you told me that."

"With the beard and wig you would have done a lot of damage to Gerard's reputation. Besides, now you won't give him fleas."

"Don't make me ice you again. We will talk of this later," she leaned over Waterfall, "To Gerard, Waterfall."

The miles sped by quickly as dread twisted in her gut. Gerard could claim any woman in the world now. Why would he need her?

She arrived two days later at his city, noting the huge swaths of nobles weaving through the streets. She recognized many she helped and others she heard of in passing.

The closer she got to the palace, the more female nobles she spotted. They whispered as she passed, snickering as she rode up the front gate of the palace.

Gerard stood at the stairs to his castle, looking weary as he turned from one family to another, talking rapidly.

"Do you really think he would look at you twice when he has all these pure blood women to choose from?"

Mary jerked around, glared at the Speaker of the Fairies.

She hovered, looking beautiful in a fancy dress as she continued, "He is a king. You are only a peasant mage. What could you ever offer him? You have no money, no stature, no family."

Her heart ached, each barb stinging as she turned back to the crowd.

Most weren't worthy of Gerard, but here and there, Mary saw women who fit a king better.

Mary admitted perhaps he saw her with a child and he merely congratulating her.

"Waterfall, we aren't needed here," Mary refused to look at the Speaker.

She knew the Speaker would be smirking.

Waterfall resisted, "You can't. He's your love."

"My mother once told me if you love someone, you must be willing to see them happy, even if it is not with you," Mary hated it to the depths of her soul.

She wanted her happy ending with Gerard.

She forced Waterfall around, wanting to flee before her determination broke.

"Please settle down," she heard Gerard saying in his calm kingly manner, "I will speak with each..."

"King Gerard, are you well?" A guard asked with alarm.

Earth shot up, cutting off her escape, making Waterfall rear in surprise.

She stared at Gerard's elemental, confused.

Screams and shouts echoed around her in fear.

"Stop this immediately," Gerard barked.

Mary looked back to Gerard as he towered over all the the women, his elemental also part of the barrier between him and the crowd. Many people ran in a panic, some huddled.

"I will have my say now you've bombarded me with marriage requests. None of you wanted me when I couldn't sire a child and when

I went to ask for the hands of your daughters, sisters I was turned aside. You isolated me," he snarled menacingly.

Mary blinked, stunned he looked less like a champion of good, but a villain about to cut loose.

"Now I'm whole, you come thrusting girls at me as if the only thing keeping you away was my ability to get children. You disgust me," he growled.

Her stomach twisted as she leapt from Waterfall, intending to stop him, to preserve his reputation.

She paused at his next words.

"The woman I will marry broke this infertility curse on myself and hundreds of others. She faced the Snow Witch with bravery, will and faith," walls erupted from the ground forcing people to part in a line to Mary.

Her heart thudded as Gerard strode down the corridor towards her.

"She gathered allies to execute her clever plan. She travelled for months to accomplish her goal and still had goodness left over to help everyone who crossed her path. She saved a powerful mage cursed worse than myself by seeing what no one would have seen."

Gerard ascended the steps to stand before Mary.

"She claimed my heart with her determination to save a single child from a foul fate, and today she stands here free of her past."

He knelt before her, making the Speaker sputter.

"Lady Mary, would you agree to marry me, to protect our kingdom together and raise children?"

She cried as she rasped, "Yes."

He stood, took her hand and put it in the crook of his arm, "We have much to talk about."

Mary realized what he meant by free from the past.

She touched her ear and found the fairy earring gone.

"Yes, your debt to my kingdom is gone."

Mary looked to the peasant fairy, only now he dressed as befitting a king. Hovering beside the Speaker, he made her look the lesser fairy.

"King Zali," Gerard bowed his head, "A pleasure to see you outside your kingdom."

Mary frowned as Zali grinned, "I am pleased I could be here to see you married finally. We both are free of the curse which left us lepers among royalty."

Mary's head whirled, "You were cursed by the Snow Witch?"

"Oh yes. My people rescued me at the same time as Gerard from the Snow Witch's clutches. I am grateful you found a way to aid my people without breaking your word about setting foot in my lands. I wish you a long and happy life together, King Gerard and Queen Mary."

Gerard leaned into Mary, "I think it best we retire from these prying eyes, my love. I have a long list for us to explore," he whispered some suggestions into her ear.

She flushed, "That may make me forget my grudges with you."

He smiled, his darker side flashing briefly, "I look forward to making you forget everything except how much we love each other."

They walked into the palace together.

About the Author

The author co-habitats with multiple, overburdened bookcases.

With twenty years of writing as a hobby, gleefully coaxing friends and family to review each new story, the author finally finished the first book for the public to pick up.